Praise for *Report from a Place of Burning*

"*Report from a Place of Burning* is utterly ori[ginal], [a] work of a master of the traditions of storytell[ing.] exquisite but also precise, George Looney un[ ] that culminate in a haunting and moving whole. With such vivid and earthly, but also dreamlike, imagery, he invites the reader to experience these accumulating revelations, casting a spell as much as offering a tale. But as lyrical as it is, make no mistake: this is a real story, one you won't mistake for an experiment. Even as you'll want to linger over the sentences, so musical and striking, and consider the brilliance of this careful and unusual construction of a novel, you'll want to turn the page, breathless for what's next. This is that rare, wonderful sort of fiction that casts a spell, fills the reader with admiration for the writer's tale[ ]
—Laura Kasischke, winner o[ ]
Award

"Looney's novel introduces R[ ] [An]derson, escorts them into our 21ˢᵗ century, and invites them to sing. And sing they do. A gyre of desire and devastation, vision and transfiguration, *Report from a Place of Burning* dazzles."
—Ann Pancake, author of *Strange as This Weather Has Been*

Gorgeous. Haunting. Unforgettable. Like every real mystery, *Report from a Place of Burning* lives on, creating questions and leaving one hungry for answers. Looney's novel smolders with captivating voices, shocking possibilities, and private histories of characters whose heartache, loss, and love are seared behind my eyes."
—Aimee Parkison, author of *The Petals of Your Eyes*

"A fabulous mix of the arcane and ordinary. A familiar Rust Belt setting—a defunct Heinz factory with the acrid smell of vinegar

lingering in the air—gives the story a desperation and Philip Dickish, dangerous, dystopian feel . . . the perfect surreal setting for this bleak (although at times, quite humorous) narrative and concoction of strange events. . . . In a profound way [the novel] speaks, metaphorically, to "the times." Amidst all the preoccupation with apocalyptic/Armageddon books/television/movies, the sense of impending doom in every facet of the news, and the rough beast that has slouched his way into the White House, here's a nod to something that passeth all understanding, with a Julian of Norwich ending of radical optimism, in spite of grim, horrific events."
—Sara Pritchard, author of *Crackpots*

"These eighteen interlocking monologues have the mysterious weight and strength of a chorus, twining and buzzing with strange harmonies. Individually, there are stunning, unforgettable moments, which build on each other in a way that creates a novel, but a novel in five or six dimensions."
—Dan Chaon, author of *Ill Will*

"The towns in this world are losing their edges; there are deer in the Heinz plant and clues in the many voices. All manner of blessings and curses live in *Report from a Place of Burning*, a poet's novel."
—Ron Carlson, author of *The News of the World* and *Five Skies*

Report
from a
Place of
Burning

Also by the Author

Fiction

Hymn of Ash (2008)

Poetry

Hermits in Our Own Flesh:
The Epistles of an Anonymous Monk (2016)

Meditations Before the Windows Fail (2015)

Structures the Wind Sings Through (2014)

Monks Beginning to Waltz (2012)

A Short Bestiary of Love and Madness (2011)

Open Between Us (2010)

The Precarious Rhetoric of Angels (2005)

Greatest Hits 1990-2000 (2001)

Attendant Ghosts (2000)

Animals Housed in the Pleasure of Flesh (1995)

Report from a Place of Burning

A Novel

GEORGE LOONEY

Leapfrog Press
Fredonia, New York

Published in 2018 in the United States by
Leapfrog Press LLC
PO Box 505
Fredonia, NY 14063
www.leapfrogpress.com

Printed in the United States of America

Distributed in the United States by
Consortium Book Sales and Distribution
St. Paul, Minnesota 55114
www.cbsd.com

First Edition

ISBN: 978-1-948585-00-2

Library of Congress Cataloging-in-Publication Data

Names: Looney, George, 1959- author.
Title: Report from a place of burning / George Looney.
Description: First edition. | Fredonia, NY : Leapfrog Press LLC, 2018.
Identifiers: LCCN 2018020620 (print) | LCCN 2018022742 (ebook) | ISBN
9781948585019 (e pub, kindle) | ISBN 9781948585002 (paperback : alk. paper)
Subjects: | GSAFD: Mystery fiction.
Classification: LCC PS3562.O597 (ebook) | LCC PS3562.O597 R47 2018 (print) |
DDC 813/.54--dc23
LC record available at https://lccn.loc.gov/2018020620

for Bowling Green, Ohio, all its ghosts and lost places

Acknowledgements

The following chapters of this novel appeared in the journals cited.

Permafrost: "The Prophet, the Gorge, and the Red Diver" (compilation of the chapters "The Prophet and the Signs," "The Prophet and the Gorge," and "The Prophet and the Red Diver" combined into one story)

Contents

Love needs to be set alight
again and again, and in thanks
for tending it, will do its very
best not to consume us.

—William Matthews

The Widow Considers Edges

THERE ARE THINGS WE SEE that have to shatter something. This I believe.

The deer that wandered onto the old Heinz plant, for one. Used to be you had to live at an edge of town to have any expectation of deer, but this town is losing its edges. Developments, they call these havens of the same house over and over, labyrinths that would've lost the Minotaur itself. Before he passed, my husband drove us into one, just to see what was what. Not only the houses were the same but the roads too, and all the sad-looking saplings, the developer's idea of replacements for what had been torn out of the earth to put up these ghosts of neighborhoods, these rumors of places where people might be said to live.

●　　●　　●

No one had moved in yet the day we drove around and around on perfectly smooth streets. Even the street names were no help. There'd be a Street and a Road and a Drive and a Circle, all with the same name. We started to pretend we'd taken a wrong turn somewhere and entered, as Rod Serling used to say, The Twilight Zone.

In that house, I said, there's a man without a face. He's lived forty years without a kiss.

15

Report from a Place of Burning

Not possible, Ray said, and leaned over to kiss me. Ray was like that, even after all our years together.

Not in front of the poor, suffering, faceless man, I said.

Not to mention his wife, Ray said and laughed, and kissed me.

And in this house, I said—pointing at a house identical to the one in which the faceless man was feeling his way to the bedroom where his wife waited for the incredible pleasure of his hands, which were all he had to make up for his lack of a mouth, for the lack of a tongue or a way to tell her how beautiful she was, which of course only his hands told him anyway, as he had no eyes to see her with— consider the case of the man who lives, literally, day to day.

Every morning he wakes a clean slate, I said. Ray was grinning. Through the course of each day he meets his wife, falls in love with her, courts her, wins her love and relishes it like a Labrador rolling in fresh-mown grass. Every night, I said, he falls asleep with his arms around this woman he loves with all his heart, and every morning he wakes up with a woman he doesn't know but is drawn to. Maybe he believes they were lovers in an earlier incarnation. Maybe he tells her this, sometime around breakfast, every day.

And what about her? Ray said. What does she believe?

It's not so much what she believes as what she fears, I said. She's terrified of the day he'll wake up with her name on his lips.

Why is she afraid of that? Ray said, his grin getting ready to become a sound.

Because, I said in my best Rod Serling, once he leaves The Twilight Zone, she'll become familiar to him, and familiarity, after all, breeds contempt.

Don't I know it, Ray said, and laughed at my melodramatic hurt face.

Still, we were lost in the sameness of what someone had named Sycamore Hills. We were no more than three miles from the house we'd lived in almost thirty years, we knew that. But it didn't feel like we were that close to anything we knew or could call ours. And where we were there were no hills, and not a sycamore in sight. Just

The Widow Considers Edges

the same house and the same yard and the same sidewalks, over and over.

Finally, for your edification, Ray said in a much better Rod Serling than I could muster, consider the case of the woman who believes the dead speak to her. Consider how, as a girl, no more than twelve years old, her heart stops in her chest. Watch her frantic mother and father work over her, crying, the father breathing into her little mouth, the mother pressing in rhythm against her thin chest. Now see her taking a breath on her own, her heart starting up again, and see how the mother and father hold her.

Now look into her face, Ray intoned in a voice too deep for even Serling. See that something's missing. I couldn't help but shiver, knowing, I was sure, what was coming. This twelve-year-old girl is suddenly not twelve, Ray, as Rod, said. She knows something didn't come back. And now see how she seems to be listening to something the mother and father cannot hear. Listen. Can you hear it? The voices of those on the other side, those who stand beside what didn't come back. That which was in the heart of the twelve year old girl but is now with them.

You are now leaving The Twilight Zone, I said, pointing to the turn which we'd taken into the labyrinth.

Darn, Ray said. Now we'll never know what happens to the woman who listens to the dead.

Don't worry, I said. I'll tell you later.

I never did tell him. I couldn't bear to, knowing that, alive, he could never have borne it.

•   •   •

All the edges of town are being lost. The deer's woods are being torn up and hauled away, so they're venturing further into town. What's left of the Heinz plant is just across the street. Thirty years ago or so, when the plant was built, it was the edge of town. The town grew right around the plant and kept going. The house Ray and I lived in for most of our married life, the house I've stayed in, was one of the few built here before the plant opened. The porch I sit out on and knit on good days used to face woods. Now there are just these old maples, in rows, lining the streets, and every year crews from the city go up and down the street and trim back branches from the power lines. This can't be good for the trees, I've always thought.

When we first moved in, the plant was operating at full capacity, three shifts day and night. We had to get used to the smell. The constant odor of vinegar wasn't the worst. The worst was a smell we could never name.

Ray once said it was the smell of a magician who died in the midst of one of his tricks. This magician, Ray said, was such a great magician and people so believed in him that they were sure they saw him emerge from the trunk that had been submerged in the tank of water. The people applauded, gave him a standing ovation, in fact, and went home, all of them talking about that last trick, how amazing it was, asking one another, How did he get out of that trunk?

How did he do it? people asked one another for weeks afterwards. Even his assistant couldn't believe it, though she believed he did and saw him taking his bows before the crowd of standing people, applauding him. She even felt his strong hand take hers and raise it up and swing it down for the final bow. But no one took down the last trick. The crew had all been so impressed they went and got drunk and stumbled through town singing dirty songs and chasing women and little girls until the sheriff forced them to leave town.

The tank stood there, Ray said, in the middle of the town's park, and the body of the magician rotted inside the trunk submerged in the water that itself grew rancid with algae and clotted by mosquitoes and so was avoided by everyone but a few boys who wrote things on it with magic markers, names and hearts and words they weren't supposed to know, Ray said.

Another time, it was the smell of a barge of garbage no city anywhere in the world would accept. Ray said the town council had taken a bribe to allow it to be dumped under the town, in the sewers. He'd heard it killed the rats and the baby gators that had lived down there, and all the rotting vermin added their own putrid stench to the odor of the garbage itself. This was a particularly bad day, long before the fire. No one sat on their porches that day.

Most days weren't that bad, and by the time of the fire, we hardly noticed the smells from the plant.

•   •   •

Some days I could swear there's vinegar in the air. Is there such a thing as ghost odors? They say that people who lose limbs can sometimes still feel a pain where there's nothing at all. Phantom pain they call it. Can a place be haunted by a phantom odor? Is that what lured the deer?

It had wandered into what used to be a walkway between buildings. It was one of those walkways with a sidewalk that crossed through it. The deer had gotten in following the crossing sidewalk and panicked, the way I've seen birds do. They fly into the walkway and seem to forget how they got in and start flying against the windows that line the brick structure. At least a dozen times over the years Ray and I crossed the street in the evening to help a bird get out before it bashed its little head against the glass one too many times. More than once, I held some sparrow or wren or finch in my hands and carried it out of the walkway and let it go. Times we didn't see them, the birds would be swept out and thrown away, having martyred themselves against the glass.

There was no way I was going to lead that deer out. I knew it. I could hear its hooves on the glass of the windows and the concrete and the brick. It was leaping and pawing the walls and windows in fits. It would lie down for minutes and I'd almost get to thinking about something else, and then it was up again and leaping from one wall to the other, bumping up against the glass and scraping it with its hooves until it wore itself out and laid back down.

Report from a Place of Burning

This must have gone on for nearly half an hour before some boys I think lived on the next street saw it. They were throwing a baseball among the three of them and moving down the street, heading for the park a few blocks away no doubt. One of them saw the deer and shouted to the other two. The three of them walked up the sidewalk from the street that led through the walkway. They were laughing, but I had no idea what they were going to do. I was watching from the porch and could have yelled to stop them had I known.

The one with the baseball, laughing, threw the ball at the poor deer. It must have hit the deer, because it went wild, leaping against those walls and windows and not stopping. The boys backed off, and when I yelled at them they started to run. The damage was done, though. The deer was absolutely frantic, smashing itself against the windows. Several started to crack and then the deer leaped again and went right through one of the windows. There was a sparkling around it as it came through, glass shards reflecting the sun. It was almost magical, and I try not to think of what must have been left in the flesh of that deer, which took off down the road and was soon gone.

The image of the deer in the moment it came out with the glass all around it glittering stays with me.

•   •   •

When I was a girl, my brother used to tease me something awful. More than once, he'd get me trapped in a corner and tickle me till I was heaving. Once, he kept me huddled in the bathroom while he hit me over and over with a Nerf ball. Every time it hit me in my side or in my leg I'd laugh and cry at the same time. If I could have, I'd have leapt through the bathroom window and sparkled in the glass like that deer.

Or like the stained glass window my brother shattered.

My brother was always getting into trouble. He was caught streaking at school, for instance. He and three other boys streaked through the gym during a basketball game, with all the parents in the stands. They ran naked, except for shoes and socks, onto the court, and two of them, my brother being one, grabbed a startled cheerleader and carried her out with them. She ran back in a minute later, laughing. Later I heard how they'd made it all the way to the classroom where their clothes were and were getting dressed when the vice-principal and a couple of teachers found them. They were suspended for two weeks, not that they cared. They were legends.

The stained glass window fiasco resulted from the fact that one of the places my brother and his friends would drink was the woods just behind the Episcopal church in town. My brother would heist beer while he was supposed to be mopping the floors at the IGA and stash it outside when he took the empty cola bottles out to the alley where they were kept till they were picked up by the bottler. Then he'd drive to the church parking lot and take the beer into the woods where his friends would join him and they'd get drunk and then head downtown to the Dairy Queen where they'd pretend to fight and harass any girls who came for ice cream.

One night someone left the lights on in the church. I heard about this from one of my brother's friends. My brother's always denied he had anything to do with what happened. What his friend said was that when they came out of the woods and my brother saw the stained glass figure of Christ Healing the Lepers all lit up, he started shouting.

Your brother, his friend told me, just went off. He was cursing at the figure in the window, and, his friend said, I swear he started crying in the midst of the curses. It was like he was so angry he could barely be bothered to form actual words. It got to the point that, whether it was the beer or his crazy anger, his words were so slurred together it was like he was, as they say, speaking in tongues. At one point, he ripped his shirt off and flung it in the air in the direction of the window. I tried to calm him down, his friend said, and he knocked me to the ground and was going to kick me when he stopped and turned and ran off, ranting, toward the church.

Report from a Place of Burning

Just outside the door to the church he bent down and picked something up, his friend told me. None of us followed him, so we don't know for sure what it was. It must have been a rock. There were always some pretty big rocks there under the evergreen bushes near the steps up to the door of the church. It must have been one of them.

Whatever it was, he took it into the church with him. We could hear him still yelling inside the church, but we couldn't make out what he was yelling. We could tell he was angry though. Then we heard the crash and saw the shards of the stained glass figure of Christ leap out into the night air, gleaming, reflecting the light from inside the church.

We'd been drinking, but we all knew this was something none of us would ever be able to explain. The way that figure of Christ shattered into what almost seemed fireworks. It was awful, and it was beautiful. We knew he'd broken something he ought not to have broken, but it was almost as though he'd broken that stained glass window to give us that moment of glittering beauty.

It was something, he said. Really something to see.

•   •   •

Ray, when he was alive, could break just about anything. God love him, he tried to be handy, to fix little things around the house. Every now and then he did. We celebrated those small salvations like they were national holidays. We'd take off and stop and buy some beer and head for the drive-in, or we'd go to some ridiculously expensive restaurant and have steaks and champagne.

More often than not, though, we'd have nothing to celebrate. I remember once a crazed blue jay broke its bright body against the living room window and it cracked. After burying the blue jay, Ray visited the local hardware store. They sold glass, sheets of it to fit into the frames of windows as large as our living room window and larger. Ray walked a sheet of glass home from the store.

People didn't know what to make of it, Ray said. A man carrying a sheet of glass through town.

The Widow Considers Edges

I peeled potatoes in the kitchen for dinner while Ray took a hammer to the cracked window, taking it out with one good swing. After that, now and then I could hear tiny scraping noises and some tiny sounds of glass shards falling to the hardwood floor under the window. The potatoes were peeled and already soaking when Ray called me to come into the living room. I barely heard him as he was standing outside when he yelled for me. When I got to the living room, I could see that Ray had gotten that sheet of glass into the frame and there was fresh putty around the edges of the glass.

How's she look? Ray yelled from outside. He was standing there grinning, his hands crossed in front of his chest, looking so satisfied with himself. I could see a little blood on the sleeves of his shirt. It hadn't gone in without a struggle, I knew.

I was just about to tell him it was like looking through air, when there was a strange sound and I watched as a crack started down from the left corner of the glass and moved diagonally, jaggedly, across and down. It was like watching the earth come apart in those cartoons where there's supposed to be an earthquake and the split in the earth separates, say, the coyote from the road runner. You've seen it, haven't you? How after the crack passes all the way across the drawn-in landscape, the part the coyote's standing on falls and we watch it fall and get smaller and smaller until it's just a dot and then there's always that puff of dust.

That crack spread down the glass from one corner to the other, and then the top of the glass, the part above the crack, slipped out of the fresh putty in the frame and slid past the lower portion and fell into the grass under the window, taking more than one reflected image of Ray with it as it fell. And taking Ray's grin along for the ride.

Yep, Ray could break just about anything, bless his heart.

• • •

Kids are playing some kind of game in the ruins of the Heinz plant. From the porch I can't make out their yells enough to know what game it is, or its rules. Even though it's hours before the sun will go down and it'll start to get dark, I don't think they should be playing over there. A few weeks ago, men in overalls and hard hats starting tearing down the plant. They came with bulldozers and other big, awkward-looking yellow machines and starting gutting the buildings. They haven't gotten very far yet. The buildings just across the street from me haven't been touched. Still, I've never liked the way the kids in the neighborhood used the abandoned buildings for fortresses and who knows what. I've worried for years a child was bound to go through a floor somewhere, or a building would collapse on a whole group of kids. I've told my concerns to my neighbors.

Kids will be kids, one said once, as if that somehow was a chant that could protect them. Kids will be kids, she repeated, going back to her garden.

Now it's got to be even more dangerous, what with the way things are being ripped up and torn down every day by the men in overalls and hard hats. But I can't do anything about it. Yesterday, I yelled at some kids from the porch, told them how dangerous it was over there. They laughed and ran further back into the plant, closer to where the machines were working. Someone's bound to get hurt.

● ● ●

Last night there was a heavy fog. From my bedroom window, up-stairs, the Heinz plant, draped in the fog, looked like one of those old paintings of Hell. There were even some small fires burning here and there in the fog.

Teenagers. They've been coming to the plant for years, to drink and make out. I know that's what the fires were, but last night they seemed to be something else. Something terrible. Usually, thinking about what the teenagers are doing over there at night just makes me smile. Not last night. Maybe it was the fog. Maybe it was some-thing else.

The Widow Considers Edges

The strangest thing, though, was not what I saw but what I thought I saw. I was about to go to bed, the light was already out in the room, and I looked out the window as I started to get into bed. What I thought I saw was the figure of a deer, running, on fire, through the fog. Then it was gone.

This morning, the fog hadn't lifted yet. All morning, there were the cries of redwing blackbirds echoing in the fog, all the fires out.

The Adulterer Is Trapped by Dreams

TALK OF DREAMS STARTED IT ALL. From the office, where I figure the day's sales, I can hear the cooks, the two teenage boys I got stuck with for closing, breaking down the breading table in the kitchen. I know the sounds. I made them thousands of times myself before I moved up into management. Angela's alone up front, restocking the styrofoam mashed potato cups. Even doing something so mundane, there's a grace to Angela I've never seen in anyone else.

Angela's the reason I'm stuck with the two in the back. Managers have to make concessions to get the people they want to work with. In order to get Angela, I had to settle for those two. One of them's just turned the radio up. Lynard Skynard's "Freebird" is firing up back there, making it all the way out here. Angela smiles and her hips move almost imperceptible to the music. God, the way she moves. No dream could convince me more that there *are* angels in this world.

Like I said, it was talk of dreams that started things almost two years ago now. Angela had just recently started working here. She was different from the other girls. Older, for one. And married. Most of the girls that work here at Famous Recipe are still in high school, this their first job. So training new girls can be a pain. Most wouldn't even be able to spell discipline.

But Angela wasn't just older, she wasn't local. Angela was from

The Adulterer Is Trapped by Dreams

Kentucky originally. She'd grown up there and had come north to go to college. Though you couldn't tell it to listen to her. She'd lost whatever accent she might have had by the time she came to work here, after she finished college. Which is where she met her husband. She was working because he was still a student, going to graduate school in Education. So money was tight.

We hit it off pretty much right off the bat. She was the only girl at Famous Recipe who got my jokes. And we could talk for hours without once slipping into the kind of vapid, polite gargling with liquid licorice that passes for conversation around here. She'd tell me stories of growing up in Kentucky, like the time on a dare she walked, like a tightrope artist, along the slim edge of a bridge hundreds of feet above the Barren River. Of course, she'd been drinking. Drinking seemed to be involved in most of her stories.

Drinking became a part of our story, too. But not in the beginning.

At first it was all completely innocent. I know, everyone says that, but it really was with us. We just talked, about our lives, about the world, about everything. I started to pick up on certain comments Angela would make that suggested things weren't great at home, and slowly I came to realize I wanted to do more than talk with Angela. But back then I thought of myself as a moral person, not someone to get involved with another man's wife.

Even as I was falling in love with Angela, I told myself nothing would ever happen between us. That I'd enjoy her company at work and that would be that.

That's when I started arranging to have Angela's schedule mimic mine. The excuse I told myself, and the other manager, was that I liked having Angela on my crew because she was more responsible than most of the other girls. Which was true. That's why I often ended up with slackers back in the kitchen. Compromise. You've got to give something to get something. But having Angela around was worth it. Though I began to find it impossible to deny it wasn't just for conversation that I wanted her around. Still, it was

27

innocent and I believed it would stay that way. Like I said, I was convinced I was a moral person.

• • •

One night one of the girls was talking about a book she'd had to read for some class. It was a slow night. I'd already sent one of the cooks home. The one cook left had started to break things down in the kitchen, preparing to get out quickly after we closed. I could hear him banging out the beat of some Allman Brothers' tune with a spatula while the water ran in the sink. He wasn't a half-bad drummer.

The book was about dreams, and what she was saying was something about how the book said we need to dream in order to stay sane. Something about how dreams are the brain's way of sorting out all the images it's accumulated—not that she used that word for it, stored up, is the way I think she put it—over the course of a day. She said that our dreams are really just the residue—the stuff left over, as she put it—of the sorting process. From what I could gather from the snippets I heard, the idea was that dreams are a kind of toxic waste dump and without them all that waste would build up in our brains and poison us, drive us crazy.

Like I said, it was a slow night, and I'd already done most of the day's paperwork, so I came out of the office and helped the girls clean, joining in on their conversation about dreams being toxic waste dumps.

I don't dream, I told them.

Angela jumped on that right off. That explains a lot, she said, smiling. Clara, the other girl, laughed.

You don't know the half of it, I said, and laughed, maniacally, rubbing my hands together.

Angela and Clara both pretended to cringe in fear and held one another. Eek, Clara said, giggling.

Hey, Clara, the cook yelled from the back. You got a phone call. And when Clara went in the back to take her call, Angela stopped playing around, though she still wanted to talk about dreams.

The Adulterer Is Trapped by Dreams

You have to dream, she said. Just because you don't remember doesn't mean you don't dream. It just means there's some reason you don't want to remember.

I suppose you remember your dreams, I said.

Not only do I remember them, I can control what I dream about, she said.

That's impossible, I said in a way that made it clear I wasn't calling her a liar.

I can, she said. If I spend some time before I go to bed thinking about something or someone, I end up dreaming about what, or who, I focused on. But I have to really concentrate for it to work, she said.

I wish I could do that, I said, not seeing where this was about to go. To this day I don't understand why I didn't.

Why? Angela said. Is there someone you'd want to dream about, if you could?

I'd been thinking, of course, that if I could control my dreams, and remember them, I'd dream about Angela. About being with her and doing a lot more than talking. The thing was, it seemed Angela knew what I'd been thinking. In fact, it seemed she had known I was thinking it before I'd realized it. That she'd led the conversation to this point.

I was feeling a lot of guilt. Not that I'd done anything wrong, though I suppose it could be argued that falling in love with another man's wife is, in itself, a wrong thing to do. What the Catholics would call a sin. Don't some Catholics believe that to imagine committing a sin is a sin? Which means every sin is actually two sins you need to confess.

God knows I'd thought of doing a lot of things with Angela, but I never intended to do any of them. How did she know? And she did know, I've learned. She's admitted she knew what I was thinking about long before this talk of dreams. She's said she doesn't think she was deliberately leading the conversation that night, but, she's said, she's really not sure. Maybe she was, she's said.

29

Report from a Place of Burning

I tried to get out of it with my usual humor. I made jokes about different actresses and political figures, and she let me off the hook until the next night.

After closing, she was stocking the front counter while I finished balancing the day's sheets.

So, who'd you dream about last night? she said, smiling.

The cooks were in the back singing along with Bob Seger's "Against the Wind," badly. I think they hit one note out of every six. And one of them couldn't even get the words right.

I don't dream, I said. Remember?

You dream, all right, she said. Come on, you can tell me. Who is it you want to dream about?

I was sure she knew. She was waiting for me to admit I wanted to dream about her, since I couldn't do anything but dream about her. Since she was married and all. She's told me she was pretty sure she knew I wanted to dream about her, but wasn't sure. She's told me she was confused by what I seemed to be thinking because she couldn't imagine why anyone would want to dream about her. It's amazing, the image some people have of themselves.

Who do you think I want to dream about? I said. Obviously you have some idea, so you tell me, who do I want to dream about?

But she refused to say anything. You're the one who wants to dream about someone, she said. I just don't know why you can't say who it is.

We'd recently starting taking walks sometimes together after work. Every night she walked her dog, Lena, a mix of Husky and something else, who looks for all the world like a wolf, but has the gentlest personality of any dog I've ever known, and sometimes I'd meet her somewhere and we'd walk several miles together, talking.

If we walk later, I told her, maybe I'll tell you.

All right, she said.

The way these walks would work is, she'd call me at the store before I left if she was going to be able to meet me. Her husband didn't know about us walking together. Even though, as I've said, it was innocent back then, she was afraid to tell him about me walking with her. Apparently, from what I've gathered, he doesn't want her to have any friends, especially men. Even though it sounds like he doesn't want to spend a lot of time talking with her, he doesn't want anyone else doing so. So I'd wait ten to fifteen minutes after locking everyone else out, and if she didn't call I'd go home. Again, as hard as it is to rationalize now, this seemed innocent.

Of course she called. Ready to confess? she said on the phone. Meet me at the corner.

Nothing happened that night. I admitted that if I could control my dreams I'd want to dream about her. She admitted she'd suspected that, and said she thought it was nice of me to say it, and then we talked about dreams and the things people are afraid of and moved gently away from the confession until she had to get back home. I walked her back as far as the abandoned Heinz plant. The apartment complex where she lived with her husband was just across some railroad tracks from the plant, a place we'd come to haunt.

I walked home alone, believing nothing was going to happen. I was, after all, a moral person. A good person. And so was Angela. Nothing was going to happen, of that I was sure. I remember cursing God that night as I walked home, because nothing was going to happen.

• • •

Sometimes I think God is just too cruel. That night as I walked home was one of those times, but not the first. Not by a long shot.

Once, back when I was still a cook, I burned myself. Bad. I hadn't been to bed the night before. I'd been up all night trying to keep a friend from killing herself. Her boyfriend had been beating up on her pretty regular for months, and had finally bruised her enough to be through with her. He'd taken his stuff and moved back in with his former girlfriend, after telling Stephanie, my friend, how worthless she was. He had her believing it, the bastard.

She'd called me, crying, and told me he'd left her and she had this bottle of pills in front of her, along with whiskey, and she wanted to take the pills. I'd gone right over and spent the whole night and most of the morning talking her out of it, trying to get her to see the guy for the asshole he was.

Why is it some women have such a hard time seeing the assholes that are right in front of them? These same women can easily spot them from the distance of other people's lives. But when they're so close to them you'd think they couldn't possibly miss seeing them, they can't see them no matter what. That's always been a mystery to me.

By the time I left her to go to work, I had the pills and she was sleeping, exhausted. I really needed to sleep, and I should have called in sick, but back then I was what they call a trooper. For the first few hours, everything was fine, but as the night wore on I was finding it harder to concentrate, to keep my mind on what I was doing. It was getting hard just to keep my eyes open.

It was a slow night. The manager had already sent the other cook home, and I was already starting on some cleaning when we got a late rush. There'd been some ball game or concert or something at the local high school, and suddenly the lobby was full and I had to get some chicken in the warmer. I breaded and dropped four pots without incident. It was when I was getting the chicken off the stove it happened.

Back then, we cooked the chicken in pots. When the timer went off, you'd pop the pressure valve on the pot and cut off the burner at the same time, wait a few seconds for the pressure to release, pop the lid and place it upside down on the rack right over the stove, then grab the pot's handle with one hand and the edge of the pot with the other, a folded rag in between your hand and the metal, of course. You'd lift the pot and bring it over to the grease table where there'd be a rack waiting for the chicken. The shortening would flow back into the reservoir where it'd be pumped through a filter into a second reservoir from which you'd refill the pot for the next round and place it back on the stove.

The accident happened at the grease table. What you're supposed to do is hit the table at just the right spot on the pot so that it makes it easy to tip the pot over onto the table, pouring the chicken over the waiting rack. Because I was so tired and not concentrating as well as I should have been, and this is the part to this day I don't really know exactly, somehow with the last pot I missed the right spot. Either I hit too high on the pot or too low. What I do know is the hot shortening splashed up over my hand when the pot hit the edge of the table, at which point I dropped the pot and more shortening splashed up and got my arm. I was not quiet about the pain. The manager came back, saw what had happened, and had one of the girls up front drive me to the emergency room.

I had second and third degree burns, and to this day there's a scar on the back of my left hand to remind me. But the burns weren't what had me cursing God that night.

After I'd been treated and was waiting in the lobby for a prescription for the pain, a woman came in, wearing some sort of sleeping gown, with something wrapped in a blanket in her arms. It was clear the woman had been crying, that she was all cried out. Her eyes were red and puffy and I don't think she could see clearly at all. I was standing in front of the desk, waiting for my drugs. The woman must have thought I was a doctor. She ran up to me and whimpered, it was almost pure animal that sound, with the word "Help" just barely recognizable. When she held the bundle out to me, one edge of the blanket fell away and I saw what was wrapped in it. That's when I cursed God.

There'd been a fire in an old house, one of those broken up into four or five small apartments for college students. The police would determine it was old, poorly insulated wiring that started the fire. This woman had been asleep when the fire started in the apartment next to hers. Probably because of the age of the house, the fire spread fast. One of her neighbors got into her apartment through a window and dragged her out half-asleep. By the time she was awake enough to think of her baby and yell his name, the entire apartment was engulfed in flames. The neighbor used a hose people watered their back yard gardens with to wet himself down and ran back in through the flames after the baby and brought it out, but it was too late.

Hysterical, the woman had run with it the five blocks to the hospital and the emergency room, where she held the baby out to me, charred black and smoking. There was nothing anyone could have done. Two nurses came out from behind the desk. One took the tiny corpse from her hands and the other put her arms around the woman and led her to one of the chairs along the wall of the lobby.

I got my pills and got out of there. I had no idea what to say to that woman, or to anyone.

•   •   •

Just last night, on the late news, there was a report on the latest in a series of mysterious deaths of babies. In the last several months, five babies have been found burned to death in their cribs. They showed a blurred photograph of the one last night. It was charred just like the one that night in the emergency room. The weird thing about these deaths, though, is that nothing else in the rooms burns. Just the babies. The parents have all found the charred bodies lying in cribs that are charred themselves, but not burned.

The police are calling them murders, and are looking for a serial murderer who's going around somehow setting fire to babies in their cribs. None of the parents, it's been reported, have heard any unusual crying. None of the parents have heard anything. No smoke detectors have gone off, and nothing else has been burned. Just the babies and the charred cribs.

On the report last night, they interviewed some guy from the college who was talking about what he called SHC, spontaneous human combustion. He said it's possible there is no killer. That these babies are just *going off,* that's the way he put it, on their own. He said there are documented cases of this spontaneous human combustion, though when pressed by the reporter he admitted that all the cases he knew of involved adults. And there weren't that many. Five in just a few months in the same town was odd, he admitted. Statistically, he said, it was virtually impossible. Certainly unprecedented.

The police, the reporter concluded, still believe it's the work of some sick arsonist, and are continuing to follow any and all leads.

What if all this is just some sick person's way of cursing God?

The Mother Whose Son Wasn't First

MY SON WASN'T THE FIRST. They told me he was the fifth. That's what the detectives said. The fifth victim, they called him. I had called him Samuel.

I woke at three that morning. That was when Samuel was usually waking up in his crib in the next room. I could always hear him. We had bought all the right hardware. We could hear him, Harlan and I, making those little noises he made in his sleep, as we fell asleep.

It's better than one of those ocean sounds machines, Harlan had said the night he'd set it up.

And it was. Listening to Samuel that night while Harlan held me made it easy to drift off to sleep. I'd been worried I wouldn't be able to sleep at all, that all the fears pressing themselves into my thoughts, all the things that could go wrong, would not let me sleep until exhaustion took over. But having Samuel's little sleep gurgles, amplified by the monitor, was enough to reassure me and let me sleep. A few months later, when Harlan and I started making love again, Samuel's sleep sounds was a better backdrop to sex than any music we'd ever tried.

I like to imagine that, when he wasn't sleeping, when he'd come awake and see the light from the hall reflecting on the birds that floated over his crib, he'd hear the sounds of our lovemaking over the monitor and relax and drift back off to sleep.

The Mother Whose Son Wasn't First

Samuel starting to cry around three in the morning would always wake me, and I'd go in and feed him and sing to him and put him back in his crib and, humming, watch till he closed his eyes and went back to sleep. This was our ritual. For months, every morning was the same. I'd come awake to Samuel making those little cries that always came before any real tears, and I'd be in the next room with my breast out before he had the chance to really get going. Sometimes Harlan would join me in Samuel's room, and he'd sing with me.

But that morning I woke to silence. It seemed strange, though it took a minute for it to dawn on me why it was strange. At three in the morning even mothers don't think as fast as they might later in the day. Where are Samuel's little cries? I thought finally. I could hear Harlan, his calm snoring, but nothing was coming from the monitor. Must be on the blink, I remember thinking. Damn. I hoped it was only the batteries, and not some problem with the wires or something inside the thing.

I got out of bed and headed for Samuel's room, still expecting to find him in those first little cries. Out in the hall was when I first noticed the odor. It smelled like someone had put some bacon grease in a pan and turned the burner on and walked outside to get a breath of air and ended up talking to the neighbor, forgetting about the pan and the grease until smoke started drifting out the kitchen window.

Who the hell's up cooking this early? I thought. Or this late, I reminded myself. Must be one of the neighbor's kids, I thought. Two of them were in college and often got home this late. Must have the munchies, I thought.

But the odor got stronger as I walked down the hall, and when I pushed open the door to Samuel's room, the door that was always left ajar so the light from the hall would keep his room from being too dark, I knew the smell was coming from the crib. Even before I turned on the light, I knew my baby was gone.

Harlan woke to my screams. I screamed for a long time, Harlan says. He ran into the room to find me sitting in the rocker beside Samuel's crib, holding the charred body of our son in my arms and screaming. Samuel was still smoldering. I ended up with second-degree burns on my arms, though at the time I couldn't feel any pain that insignificant.

Harlan called 911 from the bedroom and came back in to hold me. I was still screaming. Kneeling beside the rocker, he put his arms around me and cried while I kept screaming with Samuel there in my arms. My gown was streaked with the milk flowing from my breasts.

I was still screaming, intermittent, when the paramedics arrived, along with the police. Harlan went to let them in.

Harlan had to help the paramedics pry our son from my arms. Then he had to pretty much carry me down the hall to the living room where the detectives had settled after looking in the crib at the burned body of my son. They had made some phone calls, and it was while they were talking to us that the coroner arrived.

This was when they told us our son was apparently the fifth victim. They spoke to us in quiet tones, as if any loud noise might break us. It didn't matter to me how soft they spoke. All that mattered was that while they were speaking to my husband and I some stranger was putting my son into a leather bag and zipping it up. I saw the coroner carry the little bag past us and out the door. I got up to run after him.

That's my son, I shouted. Where are you taking my son? I have to feed him, I shouted. When Harlan held me and kept me from following the coroner outside, I screamed some more.

The detectives wanted to ask us some questions, but the paramedics insisted they had to get me to the hospital, to have the burns on my arms, which were red and cracking, checked out and taken care of. I was put in the ambulance, and Harlan got into a police car which followed us to the hospital. I wasn't screaming anymore. I just sat there in the back of the ambulance with my arms crossed just under my breasts.

The Mother Whose Son Wasn't First

One of the paramedics, I've always imagined, later told his girlfriend that it was eerie, that at one point he looked over at me and could have sworn I had a child in my arms. Must have been the light, he told her.

It wasn't the light. It was the ghost of my Samuel there in my arms. I felt him there, felt his little gums on my breast, milk flowing out the nipple and through the ghost body of my Samuel. My ghost child rode with me in that ambulance, all the way to the hospital, sucking and making those little noises he always made while I fed him. He was so hungry that night.

When they pulled me out of the ambulance and put me in a wheelchair to wheel me in to the hospital, Samuel stopped feeding. I placed him over my shoulder to burp him and he was gone and my arms were suddenly so empty I could feel the pain of the burns.

Then Harlan was beside me holding my hand as they wheeled me in. The hospital was so bright, it was like it was another world. The burns on my arms were grotesque in that light, and Harlan looked too sad to be real. Nothing could be real in that light, I thought. Nothing but sorrow.

They wheeled me to a table and Harlan helped me up onto it. A doctor came and talked to me as he rubbed something on the burns on my arms. I have no memory of what he said, but I remember thinking his face looked like it was peeling in that light. I guess he was tired. He'd probably been on call for more than twenty-four hours by the time he was rubbing that ointment over my arms. But right then I thought he needed something rubbed into his face, to keep his skin from sliding off. I reached up and touched his face. He was surprised but didn't stop me. He asked Harlan how I got the burns on my arms.

Our son, Samuel, Harlan told him. He was still smoking when she picked him up out of the crib and held him.

The doctor looked at Harlan. In that light that turned everything into something else, I can't imagine what Harlan looked like to that doctor.

39

Report from a Place of Burning

After the doctor finished with my arms, a nurse came in and wrapped them in bandages. She was pregnant, about six or seven months along, and I couldn't look at her. I closed my eyes while she wrapped my arms, and I could hear Harlan sniffling, trying to keep from starting to cry again. Later he told me he couldn't look at the nurse either.

The detectives came over after the nurse was finished. They'd been waiting on the other side of the room while I was treated.

The older detective, I think he said his name was DeGreco, asked the questions. I could tell he'd seen his share of things in that light.

Ma'am, he said, I know this is a terrible time, but I need to ask you some questions. Can you answer some questions for me?

I nodded my head, and Harlan put his arm around me. If it hadn't been for that light and the burning in my arms, I don't think I'd have been enough in this world to even hear what he was saying. Where was Samuel? was what I was thinking. What have they done with my son?

How did you come to find your son, he paused, not knowing how to put it, the way he was when you found him? he finally said.

Samuel always gets me up at three to feed him, I said. I woke up even though I didn't hear him crying, and went in and found him. I looked down at my empty, bandaged arms that were still burning despite the ointment. Harlan's arm tightened around my shoulders.

Did either of you hear anything strange before you found him? DeGreco asked.

We both shook our heads and Harlan was able to actually say, Nothing.

It's just like the other four, the younger detective said. I don't think I ever heard his name. He let the older man who said his name was DeGreco do most of the talking. I remember thinking a couple of times that he was a ghost, or an angel, standing there in that light so quiet and intense.

The Mother Whose Son Wasn't First

Once I almost asked him, Where were you when my son was burning? Why didn't you protect him? What kind of guardian angel are you? I almost said. I wonder what he'd have said if I had asked him that? In that light, anything was possible. Anything, that is, except my son.

It was Samuel's time, the angel might have said. Some burn more quickly in the flesh than most, but I was there to pull him from the flames of the body and lift him into an air no flame can feed off. All that's left of his burning, I imagine the angel, who was no angel but a detective seen in the light of that emergency room, saying, is in your arms.

DeGreco looked over at the younger detective when he said that, about the other four. I caught a glimpse of the look he gave the younger detective, that distorted angel. It was a look that clearly said, Not now. I guess he figured there was no room in that light for any additional sorrow.

What time did you put your son in his crib? DeGreco asked.

We put him down about eight, Harlan said. And my wife fed him again around eleven when he woke up crying. I changed him when she was done feeding him and put him back into his crib and we sang to him for about ten minutes or so. Then we went to bed. He was okay when we went to sleep, Harlan said. We could hear him over the monitor.

So, DeGreco said, at around eleven-thirty everything was fine, and you didn't hear anything strange before your wife went in to feed him at three this morning?

We were asleep, Harlan told him. No, we didn't hear anything.

Do you have smoke detectors in your house? DeGreco asked.

Of course, Harlan said. I just nodded. There's even one in Samuel's room. It never went off.

The doctor came back with a prescription for the pain in my arms, and DeGreco thanked us and told us he'd be in touch. He left with the younger detective who had never been an angel, not really.

Report from a Place of Burning

. . .

Before Samuel was taken from us, Harlan and I used to take him for walks every night. I was on maternity leave from my job at the insurance company where we both worked. The plan had been that after Samuel was in pre-school, I'd start back with limited hours, until he was in school. Harlan had to go to work every day, but when he got home we'd both take walks with our son.

Sometimes we'd just walk around our neighborhood. Our neighbors would stop weeding their gardens or mowing their lawns and come over and smile at Samuel and ask how we were making out. We got all kinds of advice. Some of our neighbors were considerably older. As I said, some had kids in college already.

Those walks were important to us. We wanted our son to know from early on how important it is not to forget the world that's around us. We wanted him to form a desire to get to know it. Knowledge, we thought, is the way to love, and we wanted Samuel to love this world.

Sometimes we'd strap Samuel in his carrier and strap the carrier in the back seat of the Honda and drive twenty minutes or so to one of those parks with some actual woods, with wood chip walking paths where people walk their dogs and some go jogging. If you go at the right time, when there aren't a lot of people there, and you take one of the longer walking paths, you can get far enough into the woods to imagine you're not in a park in a city, but in the forest. Harlan and I loved to take those paths and get as deep into the woods as we could, where we couldn't hear the traffic sounds from the nearby interstate. We'd listen to the birds and imitate their sounds and Samuel would smile at the strange sounds coming from his parents' mouths.

There were deer there, and several times we saw them from a distance, chewing on leaves or just standing in the mottled light. Every time we saw them, whichever one of us had Samuel on our back would turn around and the other would point to the deer and whisper to Samuel, saying, Look at the deer. Samuel always made the same sound when he saw deer, the sound a slow-draining sink makes as it finishes draining but with a vowel sound in it, a long u sound gurgling with the water down the drain.

Once, Samuel made that sound behind us. When I turned around to ask what he was saying, I saw two deer not four feet away from us, crossing the path. Samuel made his deer sound again and the two deer stopped and looked at us. I whispered to Harlan not to move, and we stood there as still as we could while Samuel went on making his deer sound and the deer stood frozen on the path. Then one of the deer sniffed at the air and Samuel made his deer sound again and the deer turned toward us and took a couple of steps. The deer was looking at Samuel, her ears shifting every time Samuel made his deer sound. She took another step towards us. She couldn't have been more than a foot away. Her black nose looked like it was carved out of onyx, but it moved as she sniffed the air for the smell of our child, who was smiling and making his deer sound and holding out his little hands for the deer. If it hadn't been for some kids coming down the path scaring the deer, I believe the deer would have let Samuel touch her. It was really something.

Samuel loved the woods, and it seemed the woods loved him. Harlan and I would sit out there until the light started to fade, talking about the future and making bird sounds and chipmunk sounds for Samuel. The world seemed so safe, somehow, in those woods. We haven't been back there since Samuel was taken from us. Sometimes, even the sounds of the wrens and robins and cardinals around our home drive me to tears.

•   •   •

Since Samuel's death I've taken up painting again. Back in college I used to paint. It's how I met Harlan. He was a model for a life studies class I took. It was a joke with us, that after I bagged Harlan, after he was mine to touch and hold, I didn't need to paint him anymore. The real reason I stopped was time. First, my job. Breaking in as an insurance adjuster at even a decent-sized company requires more time than just a nine to five schedule. Once we were both settled in our jobs, Harlan and I started talking about having a family and set out to get me pregnant with Samuel. And after Samuel was born, of course, all my time was devoted to him.

Life gets in the way of what we see ourselves as never giving up. We fool ourselves, though, tell ourselves we'll get back to whatever it is. In my case, I never threw away my artist's supplies, or put them out on the lawn with other things we never used anymore to sell for cheap to neighbors or couples driving by who slow and stop and park just up the street and walk back to see what they can get for what little they have.

Two weeks after the funeral, after they placed the small casket with what was left of Samuel into the ground, I started painting again. Finally I had the time. There was no way I was ready to go back to work, no way I'd be ready for some time. Harlan and I weren't walking together when he got home in the evenings. We sat in front of the television and barely spoke. He'd order in pizza or Chinese, and we'd watch Vanna turn letters over or Judge Stone talk to his black and white of Mel Torme or make some bad pun based on some strange case brought before him. Game shows or silly comedies, nothing where anything of consequence would happen. There's no room in our lives for any more of that.

During the days I paint. I started with several small canvases, but before anything was finished I'd stretched three large canvases and started in on those as well. It's a series I'm working on. The first one I finished is actually one of the larger ones, a canvas four feet by six. The whole canvas is engulfed in flames, but it's not Samuel I've painted. Samuel is nowhere in this canvas. There's the vague hint of some kind of structure being enveloped by the fire. Maybe it's the Heinz plant. I worked on that fire, the one a few years back that shut down the plant. I headed the team that walked through the burned out plant looking for the cause of the fire. Maybe that's what I've painted. The fire that was there before I was. That's what I told Harlan. It's the fire at the Heinz plant.

Harlan's not sure it's a good thing, what I'm painting. He hasn't come in to look at the canvases since I showed him the first one, the fire at the Heinz plant. He noticed the other canvases, the various beginnings of conflagrations. Maybe it seemed like the whole room was on fire. I guess it was too much for him. Though I'd like to know what he would think of that first canvas now. I've worked on it since he saw it and walked out of the room without a word. In the right corner of the canvas, headed in towards the center, is a figure barely discernible, wrapped in flames as it is. I'm not sure, but it could be a deer, a deer on fire running toward the center of the blaze, as if at the center there could be some kind of salvation. What would Harlan say if he saw this burning deer? What do I want him to say?

The Detective Questions His Methods

DON'T TAKE IT TOO PERSONAL, KID, DeGreco tells me.

But I've been to the corner diner downtown at six in the morning and seen the retired cops staring into their coffee, mumbling about this or that case, how all they needed was one little slip-up, some bit of physical evidence, or even an eyewitness who hadn't been drunk or high at just the wrong time. I've seen firsthand what an unsolved case can do. And the cases those lost souls mutter about the most, the ones that wake them at three in the morning and won't let them back to sleep, that leave those little tics in the muscles of their faces, the one thing those cases all have in common is they involve children.

I've seen DeGreco's face already developing a twitch, and DeGreco's seen it all. Hell, he's nearly a legend.

When I was brought in to the Captain's office and told I'd be working with DeGreco, I almost asked if he was still alive, I'd heard so much about the guy. So you know if it's getting to DeGreco it's got to be bad.

Don't take it personal, he says. Good advice, if impossible. I mean, when babies are going up in flames one after another all over town and we don't have clue number one, how do you not take that personal?

Maybe it was bad luck, my getting assigned to work with

The Detective Questions His Methods

DeGreco. The only reason I'm on this case is because they had to give a case like this to him. He is a legend, after all. Me, I'd just as soon be tracking stolen vehicles than looking for the sicko who's going around setting fire to babies. This is just too weird. And the people I've had to talk to for this case already. I could write a book.

Yesterday was a bad one. One of the worst so far. DeGreco and I got the call a little after 3 AM. We had just pulled in to the Big Boy out by the mall and placed an order for a couple of coffees and a Danish for me and, for DeGreco, his usual, a fried egg sandwich. Not that it's on the menu at Big Boy. But DeGreco, remember, is a legend. For him, they make things up special. His fried egg sandwich, for instance, isn't just a fried egg between two slices of bread. No. It's more complicated than that.

That's one of his lines, actually. We'll be working on a case and I'll come up with what I figure has got to be the answer and, without thinking, if I thought about it I'd know enough to keep my mouth shut, I'll tell DeGreco what I've come up with and he'll just smile that odd smile of his and shake his head so slightly if you weren't paying close attention you wouldn't even see it and say, It's more complicated, kid. I've only been working with DeGreco a little more than half a year, and I've already heard that phrase enough it sometimes wakes me in the middle of the night.

A DeGreco fried egg sandwich is a complex melding of flavors and textures. First, the bread has to be sour dough rye, and it has to be grilled, in butter. The fried egg itself is actually two fried eggs, and the yolks have to have been broken just about 30 seconds before taking them out of the skillet and setting them on the bread, along with a slice of cheddar cheese and a slice of provolone, and two slices of bacon, crispy. Of course there's the mayo and the brown mustard which have to be laid down before the eggs.

DeGreco is precise in his instructions. He needs things he can control, things he can have some say over, to be just so, and to be just so every time. There ain't much in this world you can count on, kid, DeGreco likes to say as he holds his fried egg sandwich up and prepares to take a bite. What you can count on, he says, make it something you like.

He'd only gotten two bites down when the call came in over the radio. They don't use numbers for these calls anymore. No number seemed enough, so they just come on the air and ask for DeGreco and, when he answers, the dispatcher, usually Elaine, just says, Another fire in the crib, and gives us the address. With yesterday's, there have been five so far. Five babies burned to char in their cribs, while the cribs themselves had minimal damage and nothing else in the rooms where the babies were sleeping was touched by the fire at all. Two of the babies burned in their cribs in the same room the parents were asleep in, the crib not more than six feet from the bed where the mother and father slept.

The lab reports have been just as strange, just as puzzling, just as frustrating, as the crime scenes. You'd think for a baby to burn like that there'd have to be some kind of accelerant used that would leave traces on the blackened little corpse, but with each of the four the lab work has come up empty. No gasoline, no turpentine, no lighter fluid, none of the usual suspects, as they say. No evidence that anything was poured over the babies to help them burn, and nothing was found in the rooms where the bodies were that could have been used to start a fire. How can these babies just be burning up like this?

Nothing about these cases makes any sense. If a baby were set on fire, you'd expect it to make some noise over something like that wouldn't you? You'd expect it to be crying like there's no to-morrow. At several of the crime scenes, the parents had monitors set up. You know, one is left in the room where the baby is and the other the mother or father carries around while they do chores or just get a little rest. They can hear their baby when it moves around or cries out, that's the thing, and if the baby started crying they would hear it and head in to see what needed to be done. Certainly, if their baby were burning alive on the other end they'd hear something.

The Detective Questions His Methods

But in each case, no one heard any sounds to suggest anything was wrong. They just found the charred bodies in the morning still smoldering, still smoking in the rooms with smoke detectors, placed on the ceilings often right over the cribs, that never beeped at all. How can a baby burn to death and not only not be heard but not set off the smoke detector that should have woken anyone in the house no matter how sound a sleeper they may be? Don't even get me started on the ones who burned up in the rooms with the parents not six feet away.

DeGreco told me to drive. He wanted to finish his sandwich. My Danish, I guess he figured, wasn't anything special. It could wait. Driving, I let myself hope this would be the time the perp screwed up and left us something we could nail him with.

I didn't, of course, say that. If I had, DeGreco would have ripped me a new one.

First, for the hoping. Hope is not one of DeGreco's lines. Hard work, he likes to say, is the only remedy for hope.

Hope, DeGreco has said, likes to lie on the couch and tell his wife, a small woman who is always nervous and flinches at her husband's slightest motion, to For crissakes get up off your fat ass and get me a beer. It was late when DeGreco told me that and he'd thrown back a number of shots and was beginning to feel the whiskey kick in.

When he's really feeling the whiskey, he recites poetry. Yeats is one of his favorites, it seems. Several times I've heard him yell "Things fall apart; the center cannot hold. Mere anarchy is loosed upon the world." He usually doesn't get any further than this cause the crowd in the bar we hang out in after work doesn't want to hear poetry. They'll give him a couple of lines just cause he's DeGreco, and a legend, but that's all they'll stomach.

The second reason he'd have ripped me a new one if I'd said out loud what I was thinking is that he hates all the shorthand terminology everyone gets off of *Law and Order* or one of the *CSI* series. I've learned not to say perp, for instance, around DeGreco.

Report from a Place of Burning

It seems such language is too imprecise for his tastes. We need, I've heard him say to other detectives, to get back to calling things what they are. We need a vocabulary, he says, that's up to what the world gives us to name.

Everyone nods when DeGreco goes off like this, but we all keep using the lingo as soon as we're out of earshot from him. For us mere mortals, we find it's enough. Only a god, one detective said after getting the language lecture from DeGreco, should feel the need to know the exact one and only name of everything. Of course he said this after DeGreco had left the room. We all nodded. Though I wanted to ask him, What about Adam and the story of him naming the things in the garden? I didn't. After all, I wanted to agree with him, certainly with the sentiment of his statement. DeGreco can come off as pompous.

DeGreco swallowed what was left of the fried egg sandwich as I pulled into the driveway behind the ambulance. The paramedics had already been in the house and were packing things up. There was no body with them. The older medic motioned with his head, inside. They had not moved the baby, or what was left of it, from the crib. They had to wait for us. They knew the routine. If the victim's alive, then he or she is a patient. If the victim's dead, then the body, in all its accouterments, is evidence and part of a crime scene and belongs to us. Another one for you, the medic who motioned to the house said as we headed for the porch.

Inside, we could hear a woman weeping and a man with a face that could've gotten anyone lost pointed us down the hall when DeGreco asked, Where's the body, sir?

DeGreco put his hand on the man's shoulder as we passed and whispered something in his ear. The man, the baby's father of course, did not go with us into the room but headed off toward the front part of the house. DeGreco watched him go before stepping into the room. Poor guy, he said.

I had the camera. It was only the two of us, and DeGreco was the legend, not me, so I snapped whatever he indicated. If anyone else had been in the room with us, they'd have thought I was just the photographer. As luck would have it, the kid wasn't going to be giving anyone an estimation of my value any time soon.

After taking in the undisturbed room, it was picture after picture, from every possible angle, of the crib and the body in it. The viewfinder was a godsend. Without it, I might have lost it after the first few pictures. The illusion of some sort of distance from the reality of what was still smoldering in that crib was all that kept me clicking photo after photo until DeGreco was satisfied we had enough.

Notice anything? DeGreco asked. This was his way of telling me, Stop taking pictures and start looking.

I let the camera hang over my stomach and looked around at the room I had just viewed through that little window on the camera. This time I was in the room, and it was just me and DeGreco and this smoking little corpse in the crib. Except for the occasional sound of a woman weeping that made its way down the hall to this room that was obviously the nursery of a kid who was very loved, the world at that moment could have been without sound. DeGreco had asked me a question and everything was about seeing something. Despite the fact I would've given everything I had in this world to have noticed, as DeGreco put it, something, this room, as far as I could tell, was just like the other four the two of us had stood alone in, me taking pictures to DeGreco's instructions.

I was desperate. The smoke alarm, I said, looks to be new. Turns out that it was, that the father had gone out to the local hardware store the week before the baby was born and bought the smoke detector, and put a new battery in it and stood on a ladder while his wife was asleep on the couch in the living room to attach the detector on the ceiling right over where they had decided to place the crib. What I couldn't say was why that was worth noticing.

Anything else? DeGreco said.

It was a test. DeGreco was testing me. I focused on that, on DeGreco testing me, and that let me really look at the mess in that room, that charred and smoking baby in the crib. There's no evidence, I said, of the baby doing anything in response to being burned alive. I mean, you'd expect him to grab at the edges of the crib, to pull himself up and tear at that damn crib, but there's nothing except for some charred marks around the body that seem to have been incidental, just proximity charring.

DeGreco nodded, waiting.

It took me that long to notice. I'd seen it four times before, and each time it took me a while to notice it, to remember. The arms, I said, and DeGreco put his big hand on my shoulder. Bingo, he said.

We had not released all the information about the crime scenes to the press. It was standard practice to hold something back, something only the person who committed the crime could know. Once we had a suspect, we would need this little detail to help put the sicko away. If we ever got a suspect. After five babies, we had nothing.

The baby's arms, which were little more than bone with a thin layer of what might have only been ash but was actually charred skin, were crossed on top of its chest. The baby could have just been discovered in a dark tomb in Egypt somewhere, a tiny mummy. You've seen them. Even the child mummies, the arms are crossed over the chest in a pose of, well, calm. But this was no royal child who had died and been prepared for the afterlife by hordes of priests and attendants. This was a baby who by all indications had burned to death in his crib. If this baby turned out to be like all the others, there would be no evidence indicating he had been dead before he burned up in his crib.

Everything else that was damned odd about these cases aside, this was the worst. A baby who burned to death, even if he'd been asleep when the fire started, should have woken up and been in such pain he would have torn at his crib and at himself and his charred corpse should show obvious signs of that struggle. These babies, the first four and this fifth, I was sure, even before any autopsy had been done, had died in the fire that left the cribs charred and everything else in the room untouched. In burning the babies, the fire had not set off a single smoke detector, and there was not a hint of struggle or of suffering about the corpses. The charred remains in fact, except of course for the fact they were burned, showed every sign of a calm death, a death that came to them in their sleep so quick there'd been no pain at all, just one breath then another and then nothing. The arms crossed over the little burnt chests was just another sign of this notion of a calm death.

None of it made any sense, and standing in that room which had been so carefully prepared for the child who was now just a smoking corpse in his crib, I stopped thinking like a detective and remembered something I'd seen on a recent Sunday morning on some televised church service. I had just gotten home after two days without sleep, and was too exhausted to get up and change the channel, or to find the remote I hadn't seen in days. Some very loud preacher was giving what I can only guess was his version of a sermon. He was talking about some scripture, something out of the Old Testament, back when God was a vengeful old geezer.

Then he was talking about the babies that had been going up in flames around town. God's wrath, he called it. I was up and the TV was off before I heard what I knew was coming, what supposed ill of our society he was going to blame for this fiery wrath of the almighty, this judgment enacted on the bodies of innocents.

Standing in the nursery of that fifth victim, watching DeGreco turn the charred baby over to look under the body for any evidence of who had done this awful thing, or of how it had been done, I let myself think maybe what was going on *was* Biblical. It did make a kind of sense, after all. I mean, here we were with number five, and we still had no idea how this was being done or who could be doing it. Supernatural isn't a word I'm used to using, or thinking, but it didn't seem completely out of place, especially after DeGreco pried apart the little arms and called me over.

What do you make of this, kid? he said.

Report from a Place of Burning

Another detail we would not release to the press. There, in the center of each tiny, blackened hand, DeGreco had discovered in each palm a patch of unburned skin that, surrounded by all that obscene charring, had the look of two wounds in the center of the palms. Stigmata, I knew, was what the unburned patches looked like, a kind of reversed stigmata, the entire rest of the baby's body a wound. I also knew better than to say the patches looked like stigmata. That was the last thing I should say.

Odd, was all I did say. Damn odd, I said, and snapped a couple of pictures. Was he holding something? I said, trying to be rational. Something that, though it burned finally, protected the skin it was held against long enough to leave those patches, maybe? I was trying to pull something out of the proverbial hat, I knew that, but what choice did I have?

DeGreco just shook his head.

Lucky thing, for me, the coroner picked that moment to call DeGreco on his cell phone. The coroner and DeGreco had known each other forever. Rumor is that the coroner introduced DeGreco to his now ex-wife, that they go back that far. The coroner on the phone gave DeGreco a better foil than me to work with.

Yeah, DeGreco said, though I can only guess the coroner had asked if we had another burned kid on our hands. And this one, believe it or not, DeGreco said, has stigmata. There was a pause while the coroner said something and then DeGreco almost chuckled.

Just like the others, far as I can tell, DeGreco said. What he said next caught me off guard. It wasn't so much what he said but how he said it. I had never heard him sound so human, so vulnerable.

Find us something, Roger, DeGreco said to the man who was headed our way in a black station wagon with the seal of the state and white lettering on its front doors. Anything. We need something.

By the time we walked down the hall and DeGreco had used the phone in the living room to call in and to request the lugs on this line for the last month be pulled, his humanness had worn off.

The Detective Questions His Methods

When the mother was brought into the living room, still crying, DeGreco was finishing his report over the phone and the husband, who was holding up his wife, barely, must have heard DeGreco say we had a fifth victim. Maybe the mother heard it too, but she was in such a place I doubt anything was registering but the crude fact of what had become of her son.

DeGreco spoke to the man holding onto the woman whose arms looked like they were covered with a rash. I could barely hear his voice. It was a whisper in that room at that ungodly hour.

What happened to your wife's arms? DeGreco asked.

The man explained that his wife had found their son and had picked him up and cradled him in her arms until the paramedics had managed, with his help, to pull his son, or what was left of him, what was left of Samuel, from her and place him back in the crib. Our son was still smoking, the man said. Her arms, he said, are burned.

Did your wife fold his arms over his chest? DeGreco asked the husband. The wife shook her head.

DeGreco nodded to the coroner who had come in and was standing in the hall with a leather bag draped over his arm, a demented waiter in a four-star restaurant. Everyone there wanted to be someone other than who they were, somewhere other than where they were. DeGreco gestured down the hall where the nursery was. The coroner's grin was a ghastly thing before he headed for the nursery and the still-smoking victim.

The paramedics came back into the house and one of them bent down to look at the woman's arms and told us we could, if we wanted, follow them, but that she needed to be taken to the emergency room to get the burns on her arms treated, and she had to go now. They would take her in their ambulance. You're welcome to follow, the paramedic said and, with her husband's help, got the woman, whose burnt arms were still in the pose of holding her child to her breasts to feed, up and out into the ambulance whose flashing lights changed the color and feel of the house and the yellow police tape strung up around the house and the yard. Not even the grass looked real in those flashing lights.

We waited at the hospital while the woman's arms were treated and bandaged up. DeGreco still had questions for them. He likes to cover as much as possible while things are still fresh in people's minds, he says, before memory has a real chance to get involved and start to muck things up. So I stood there in the background, hardly saying a word, while DeGreco had the couple, the mother's burned arms covered in ointment and gauze, go over again the details of how they had discovered what had happened to their child. It seemed wrong to me, a kind of torture.

This wreck of a woman, whose arms were hurting from being burned by the charred and smoking body of her son, she looked over at me while DeGreco asked her and her husband the questions he felt couldn't wait and it seemed at one point she was accusing me of something. The mother of the fifth burned baby looked at me as if I had let this happen to her son, as if I was supposed to protect him and when he needed me most I failed him. What had I been doing? the way she looked at me asked, while her son was burning up in his crib. What was more important than my baby?

I wanted to be someone who could keep babies from going up in flames. Standing in the garish light of that emergency room while DeGreco asked this couple, whose child had just gone off like a tiny Molotov cocktail thrown in his crib, questions about how it happened, I wanted to protect her. Let her alone, I wanted to say in a voice that would make even DeGreco shut up.

I stood there, mute, unable to make what had happened not have happened.

Go home, kid, DeGreco, exhausted, told me outside the emergency room doors. Let's both of us try to get some rest and start fresh on this tomorrow.

Tomorrow we'll see what the coroner has for us, he said. This time there's going to be something, DeGreco said. The freak is going to have messed up and left some sign. We just have to look for his signs, DeGreco said. It was clear he was trying to convince himself.

Funny, I thought, at home and alone except for the pretty news anchor on channel 24. The one I fall asleep with most nights. She was saying something about the farmers worrying about signs of a bad drought and they were showing the Maumee, which was low enough for the second time in the last decade, she was saying, people could walk across it from bank to bank by following the stone plateaus revealed by the drought. Isn't it funny, I thought, how DeGreco used the male pronoun, as if only a man could be doing such a thing.

What if there's no sign of him because no man, or woman, could be doing this? What then?

The Prophet and the Signs

SIGNS ARE SIGNS no matter the year.

Too many these days think mystery is antiquated, no room for it in this enlightened age. An age of reason, they call it. As if reason could overcome mystery. We may change the course of a river, but we can't predict every consequence of doing so. It might turn out the river knew, if knowledge is something a river could be said to have, better. Years after putting up the dams we may have to take them down, to return the river to the course it had chosen.

It's happening. We're beginning to see what some call the limits of our knowledge. The world, it turns out, is not mute. It's just our hearing isn't as good as we like to think it is.

Mystery isn't outdated. All of this reason so many put their faith in, and it is faith, is just another form of religion.

It's remarkable there aren't cathedrals for this new religion.

But I give science credit for understanding it's all about vision, about how things are seen. Not what they are, but how they are perceived.

• • •

Signs are signs no matter the location.

The summer of my eleventh year, I spent a lot of time playing capture-the-flag with my older brother and the kids in the

58

neighborhood. For us, this was no mere game. We spent days just setting up the battle lines and the rules of engagement. The games themselves would last a week, sometimes more. This was real, and failure had consequences.

Being captured meant you would have bruises that could take weeks to fade. Pain was something we accepted. There were nights I would not sleep, I was in such pain. But I was respected, even by the older kids. Not once did I break. No enemy ever got information from me. And when my team would release me, I'd be rewarded for my courage with a milk shake or sometimes a whole meal from McDonald's. Or they'd let me be the one to actually take the other team's flag. They'd create plans that would sacrifice others to get me in position to get the flag and get back across the battlefield home.

The battlefield often included the interstate overpass, or rather the railroad tracks under it. Those tracks ran along a gorge on one side, a place where limestone had been carved out of the earth years ago. No one was mining it by the time we lived near it. It was just an open pit, fenced in, with danger signs posted all around, and warnings against trespassing. In the spring, it would usually fill up with enough water that we would sneak through places where the fence had been cut by other kids in the past to swim in the green water. Sometimes we'd be sick for days after a swim, but that didn't stop us from going back.

It was during a game of capture the flag I saw the first sign. I'd been captured, and was being held prisoner at one edge of one of the massive concrete pillars that held up the highway. We were on the gorge side of the tracks, and they had me roped to the fence around the gorge while they interrogated me. There were two guards. One was yelling questions at me, asking where our flag was, where our forces were, what our strategy was, and the other was pounding me, his fists on my back, my arms, my chest. Sometimes one of them would slap my head or kick my thighs, but they were careful not to hurt me too much, in case they were captured in a rescue operation. There were rules in this game, like

Report from a Place of Burning

I said. It was okay to give the enemy bruises, but any real damage was punishable outside of the game. Besides, we were all friends, despite being at odds in the game, and, though the game was real to us, there were limits.

It was in the midst of my interrogation we heard shouts coming from over our heads. The guard who was pounding on me stopped and told the other guard to shut up. We heard a voice shouting but couldn't make out the words at first, nor could we see anyone. No doubt they were afraid it was a distraction for a rescue attempt, but I knew what I was hearing was not the voice of anyone on my team. It was not the voice of a teenager, of that I was certain. The three of us listened, trying to make out what the voice was saying and where it was coming from. As we listened, it became clear the voice was moving. It was getting closer.

I was the first to see him. If, in fact, it can be said I saw him. What I saw was the light reflected off the figure, a light that was captured by my eyes and burned upside down on my optic nerve. It's that upside-down, redrawn figure of light, translated by my brain into yet another unique image, I actually *saw*. I shouted and pointed out the figure to the guards. Suddenly, we were outside of the game, though they didn't untie me. There are rules, after all.

•   •   •

You've all heard the dogma. Observe and theorize. Then test the theory by observation. Again and again. The more independent the observation the better, they say. But there's the core of the deception. There's no such thing as independent observation.

There's even a scientific principle about how behind every bit of so-called science there is mystery—the Uncertainty Principle, the Heisenberg Uncertainty Principle.

For so long it was believed, yes, believed is the word, that the atom was the smallest particle of matter. Then, of course, came the realization the atom was made up of smaller particles, and they were given names. No sooner were they given names than they were believed to be made up of even smaller particles, and down the rabbit hole we went. Like a series of Chinese boxes, matter kept opening up and opening up to reveal yet smaller particles, until it all became uncertain.

It was in this observing of these tiny bits of matter the Uncertainty Principle was born. A principle about how observation, the act upon which all theory is predicated, the rock upon which the church of science is built, how that act is tainted, is impossible without acknowledging mystery. In short, Heisenberg's principle says it's impossible to know both the direction and position of any sub-atomic particle. In order to know the position of a particle in space, to observe it, what is required makes it impossible to know the direction or velocity of the particle. And vice versa. Like those dams that change the course of rivers, this little bit of "knowledge" has repercussions that ripple across every bit of what we call science and logic and reason.

One thing it means is that observation will never provide us with an understanding of the nature of matter, of the existence of things. That at the core of everything we know is something we cannot know: mystery.

•　　•　　•

The person shouting off the edge of that freeway ramp looked to be an old man with long white hair, matted, and a white beard. He was naked and had painted his entire body red. There I was, tied to a fence near a sign that warned of danger, watching a naked man wave his red arms at the sky and shout.

The first words I could make out were, For the great day of his wrath is come, and who shall be able to stand?

Being as I was only eleven, I had not yet read the Revelation of St. John. It would be years later, when I read the naked man's words in the Revelation, I would recognize this for the sign it had been. At the time, all I knew was that something was wrong. This guy was naked, yelling off an interstate overpass.

Report from a Place of Burning

What the hell? Jack, one of the guards, yelled. Hey old man, are you crazy or what?

Yeah, the other guard, Ted, added. Go put some pants on. We don't want to see your red, shriveled johnson.

I didn't say anything. Roped to that fence as I was, this scene took on a different sort of feeling for me. Suddenly, looking up at this bony, red body and its waving arms, it was like this was being acted out for me. This means something, I thought.

•　•　•

Every observation is tainted, science tells us. And all our theories, being based upon and tested by observation, are likewise tainted. No observation is independent, since every act of observation, Heisenberg realized, is an intrusive and aggressive act. The very act of observation affects that which is observed by the act of observing it. And in that act of observation, the effect is not one-sided. The thing being observed and the observer are both affected by the observation.

Anoint thine eyes with eye-salve, that thou mayest see, St. John wrote in his Revelation.

That salve for the eyes is faith, faith in the mystery at the core of our very being. Without that faith, we are blind indeed.

The other day I read how, after decades of searching, some physicists finally found direct evidence of one of those Chinese boxes within boxes, the tau neutrino. This tau neutrino is supposed to be one of the fundamental building blocks of all matter. As if we haven't heard that before.

Signs are signs no matter the nomenclature.

This is all defined by what physicists call the Standard Model of Particle Physics—their particular book of faith. This holy text says neutrinos are hurtling everywhere all the time at the speed of light. Trillions of them just passed through you. Yet, this scripture says, they have no electrical charge and virtually no mass. So, something exists that almost doesn't exist. Isn't that miraculous?

The Prophet and the Signs

But wait. What's the proof? Just what is the nature of this direct evidence? Observation, of course. This is science, after all. So, something that almost doesn't exist has finally been found by scientists who, wouldn't you know it, have been looking for it for more than twenty years. Funny how they just happened to find it.

It's like those astronomers a little while ago who found invisible tendrils of hydrogen in the huge darknesses between galaxies. One of them actually talked about how finding this invisible matter was sure evidence that the current models of the cosmos were on the right track. Again, we have the discovery, by men and women who have a particular vested interest in finding it, of something that had already been proposed and named, something that was necessary in order for their particular theories to be on the right track. Independent observation? That missing hydrogen was found because it needed to be there, and the need for it to be there exists not in the vast darknesses between the galaxies but in the minds of those who found it. Funny, isn't it, how if we believe in something hard enough and look for it long enough we find it? Everything comes down to a question of faith, you see. It's a matter of what we believe in. Or what we've heard.

• • •

I could hear horns from the highway. And the vague shouts you could tell had come out of cars that were going by without stopping. The shouts that must have been words but which were not recognizable from where we were had that trailing off effect as the cars went by. The horns were doing it too. People were rushing by this naked, old man, painted red, and honking at him and yelling at him but not stopping.

Finally, we heard what sounded like a car door shutting. Someone had stopped up there. Though we couldn't hear it, someone was trying to get the old man to come away from the edge of the overpass. The old man was standing on the railing by this time, yelling into the gorge.

Report from a Place of Burning

And there went out another horse that was red, the naked, red man shouted. And power was given to him that sat thereon to take peace from the earth, he shouted, and that they should kill one another.

· · ·

Faith, as they say, works in mysterious ways. Sometimes, all faith requires is the right element. Maybe cesium. They taught us, in school, that there are some absolutes, some things that remain constant, and most of us cling to that belief. We want there to be certainty. Perhaps we even long for it to be true, because in our hearts we find it impossible to believe in it.

Our hearts, after all, are anything but models of certainty or stability. As muscles, they practice a rhythm hardly regular. Our heart rate is in constant flux, depending on our activities and even on our thoughts, our desires. The heart, you see, is a relativistic organ, yet it has traditionally been pictured as the center of our natures. Yes, I know science tells us that the brain is the more likely candidate. The brain and the heart have been at odds, haven't they, for a long time? The mind in conflict with the body is a paradigm present in almost every human culture, often in very different ways, it's true, but used almost universally to explain human behavior, or to justify it.

The brain, too, could be said to have its reasons for wanting to believe in certainty, in absolutes, as it's not particularly stable either. Thought itself is a kind of storm that rages across the gray landscape of the brain, with storm fronts meeting and forming obsessions and forgetfulness, depending on the winds, as it were. And the brain is the one organ that cannot replenish itself. The rest of the body renews itself fully every seven years, we're told, but the brain doesn't change with the body. The brain has to cling to what it has because when it loses what it has what's been lost is lost, and that's it. The brain wants things to stay as they are.

They shall hunger no more, neither thirst any more, St. John wrote in his Revelation.

The Prophet and the Signs

The unchanging perfection the angels speak of that awaits us after judgment is something the brain longs for, fearful as it is of loss.

One of those absolutes we were all taught in school was the speed of light. A good deal of modern physics and the models of the universe all depend on that. It's a boundary that makes a lot of "knowledge" possible. Things depend on that limit. But now, it turns out, the speed of light may be no less constant than, and just as relativistic as, the beating of our hearts.

In an experiment recently, a pulse of light traveled so quickly through a chamber filled with cesium vapor that it left the chamber before it finished entering the chamber. This, of course, would not be possible if the light pulse could only travel at what's always been known as the speed of light. The speed of light, meaning there's only one speed: *the* speed. But now we have to speak of *a* speed of light, a norm as it were. The speed that light, left to its own devices, will normally travel at.

Maybe cesium excites light. Maybe it terrifies light. Our hearts are said to race when we are excited or terrified. Maybe light is the heart of being, of existence.

Even the scientists who set up the experiment can't explain the phenomenon.

Signs are signs with or without acknowledgement.

•   •   •

And then the man painted red dove off the overpass. I saw the arms of a man in a suit reach out over the edge of the overpass, grabbing at the air where the naked old man had been standing, and then I watched his fiery body fall into the gorge, getting smaller until his body hit damp rock at the bottom of the gorge. This was near the end of summer, and there'd been a drought for several months.

His body kind of flopped a little as it hit, as if it wasn't ready yet to stop moving, as if it could convince the stone to move aside so it could continue to fall, or as if it intended to just fall through the stone itself.

My guards had looked away before the body hit, and the man in the suit had his hands over his face. I alone saw the body hit the rock. I alone watched it slide under what remained of the foul water. I alone knew this meant something, though it would be years before I knew what it meant.

By then, Jack would be dead, the victim of a car wreck. Ted would be in prison, having raped and murdered a thirteen year old girl in the gorge when he was twenty-four. He drove her out to the gorge where he tore her clothes off and sodomized her before crushing her skull with a rock. When they found the girl's body, her right hand had been cut off and shoved into her vagina, clutching three rocks.

There are signs everywhere, though sometimes it takes us years to recognize them. And some we'd rather not think of.

•   •   •

It was a long time before I understood the naked old man's ruddy dive into the gorge was a sign. It took the violence of the lives of the kids I grew up with to let me see the signs that are around us, the signs I needed to learn to read.

It's the old problem of observation at work. Why do you think the beasts around the throne St. John saw were full of eyes? Before and behind, he wrote. And within.

I remember trying to tell the story of that old man's naked plunge into the gorge to the artist who tattooed my thigh a few years ago. This was in one of those places downtown with the front windows pasted over with hundreds of photographs of different body parts covered with designs done by the artists who work in the shop. The photos are all close-ups, though you can usually tell where on the body the tattoo is by the particular curve of the flesh the tattoo only partly covers.

The artist already thought I was strange, because of what I'd asked him to place on my thigh. It was an ornate design of Hebrew letters, though he didn't know what it said. He was writing the letters on my thigh and I was telling him about the old man, how his whole body had been this scarlet red and how it had been like the air was on fire when he leapt through it into the gorge.

When I told him what the man had said just before he dove off the overpass, the artist said it sounded like something out of the Bible. He'd never read the Revelation of St. John. Even if he'd known the words he was tattooing on my thigh, he wouldn't have understood what they meant.

Had I told him that what he was tattooing on my flesh was King of Kings, and Lord of Lords, what would he have thought? Would he have thought I was crazy? Would he have thought I was a fanatic? Would he have thought I was a man who could leap from an overpass into a hollow place in the earth? Would he have known I am a sign? Would he have known I'm what's inevitable?

I am what must come.

The Widower the Dead Visit

I'M NOT SO FAR GONE as some believe.

My daughters worry about me living alone. Dad, they say, you shouldn't be alone. They've talked about sharing me. Every couple of months sending me to the other's place, like a time-share. But I won't leave this house. This is where Sarah and I lived, where I took care of her as she died, and it wouldn't be right to leave her now.

My daughters, when they visit, complain about what a mess the place is and always spend some time cleaning up. I figure that's enough of a maid service. Carol, the oldest, is always telling me it's not healthy, my staying here alone.

Dad, she says, you can't really take care of this house, and you don't need all this space. She always starts off with what she must think are the practical considerations, but she doesn't stop there. Dad, don't you think it'd be better for you to get away from the memories in this place? She's of course thinking what hovers in the rooms of this house are bad memories, memories of my last wife's slow death from the cancer that burned through her body like those fires on the news every summer out west.

Sarah was quite a bit younger, and everyone, me included, was sure she'd bury me. In fact, my daughters took a while to warm up to Sarah because of the age difference. It wasn't that they had any resentment about my remarrying. Their mother had been my first wife. We had married young, right out of high school, and she'd gotten pregnant with Carol in the first few months. By the time Carol's sister came along, it was becoming clear the two of us should never have gotten married. When Chrissy was two, I moved out. So they'd had plenty of time to recover from their mother and I being apart. Not to mention my second wife. No, it was just the age thing. Sarah was sixteen years younger than me, and . . .

• • •

. . . Sarah's in the shower. I can hear the sound of the water in the pipes. Tonight we're going out to celebrate my retiring. The guys down at the Heinz plant took me out to lunch and we had a few drinks I'm still feeling the effects of. Thinking about Sarah in the shower is too much. My clothes are off before I get to the bedroom and I just throw them at the bed. The pants miss and end up on the floor. Sarah won't be happy when she sees that, but she won't see it for a while.

She's been waiting for me. Come on in, she says, the water's fine.

It's not the water I'm interested in getting in, I tell her. She laughs and pulls me in to the shower with her and starts soaping me up, getting a lather going in my chest hair and then moving the bar of soap down my body. God, she's so beautiful, and her hands feel so good . . .

• • •

. . . Sometimes it happens. It's not memory exactly. When I remember something it's different. It's in the past and I'm not. But sometimes, just briefly, I'm in the past. I know the doctors would explain it away as some trick of the brain, the result of the Alzheimer's, but what do they really know. They've never experienced it. It's no trick. Sometimes I'm in the past for a while, and then I'm back. If I told my daughters about this, they'd probably have me committed. But I'm not crazy, and there's nothing wrong with what

Report from a Place of Burning

I'm doing. I'm not living in the past. Just visiting now and then. And never for long.

• • •

I walk a lot. It keeps me in pretty good shape for a man my age. Sarah always said I had the body of a man twenty years younger than I was, which meant, she said, that being with her I was sleeping with a woman who was really a couple of years older. My walking isn't a vanity, though. I do it to keep my diabetes under control. It's a twice a day ritual, has been for over twenty years. I even have a treadmill in the bedroom. If it's raining I use the treadmill, which is facing one of the picture windows so I can watch the trees shrugging in the wind and bending under the rain while I walk. In the winter, I use the treadmill a lot, and watch birds walking over the snow, little dark flickers in the glare of white.

Sarah used to walk with me in the evenings. Mornings, I'd have to leave her lying in bed. She was not a morning person. But walking with her in the evenings was wonderful . . .

• • •

. . . We're both a little damp. My arm makes a little sucking sound on her back when I shift a little. Her hand is twirling patterns slowly in my chest hair. My right hand caresses the skin of her upper arm and my left caresses the thigh she's thrown over my lower stomach. The red on her chest and around the base of her neck is starting to fade.

What do you think started the fire? Sarah asks me. In just a few minutes, I'm going to pull her on top of me and let her slip me inside her again.

Earlier, on the news, we watched the report on the fire at the Heinz plant, where I used to work. The reporter was standing outside the plant, and behind him you could see the firefighters still spraying down the brick buildings, smoke still drifting out of the windows. There were workers standing around too, watching the smoke and the water, no doubt wondering what it would mean for them.

A breeze blows across our damp bodies from the open window. A few weeks ago, we'd been out walking, later than usual. We'd waited because it had been a particularly hot and humid day, and we thought it'd be nicer to walk in the dark after it had cooled down a bit.

We'd been spying on people, in the houses where lights were on. We'd seen people watching television and sitting at tables writing or playing cards. The people writing were writing letters to sons or daughters in jail, or lovers they were arranging to meet in hotel rooms in other cities, or letters of resignation from jobs they'd managed to stomach for thirty years but couldn't take one more day of. Those playing cards were keeping score in games that had been going on for months or even years. Or someone was losing everything.

It was in front of one of the houses already gone dark we heard it. We had to stop and listen hard to be sure what we were hearing, but after a few minutes it was unmistakable. The hushed sounds of two bodies moving atop sheets, and the faint moans that grew a little louder as we stood there. We held one another and listened to the couple somewhere in that dark house. Someone was doing something right, that's what the woman's moans were saying. Then, there was a distinctively male voice, almost a hoarse whisper but louder and more insistent, and then the dark house was quiet.

Do you think anyone heard *us*? I ask. Sarah laughs and rolls over on top of me . . .

•　　•　　•

. . . I'm not as alone as my daughters think. Though I can't tell them. They worry about this house having too many memories for me, but memories are only one thing this house contains. There are the times I'm actually in the past, and there are of course the memories of the past, but there's something else. There's the dead.

Report from a Place of Burning

Since Sarah died, I've been visited by familiar dead, and dead people I never met when they were alive. And it's not just in the house. Out walking, I'm visited too.

I've always watched people on my walks. People in their houses, working in their yards, people driving by in cars. It always struck me that with their windows rolled up, people in cars often have a tint to them that almost makes them look the way ghosts are often made to look in movies. But now, sometimes the cars that go by while I'm walking don't just have drivers who look like ghosts, they have riders in them who are dead.

Just last week a car went by, slowing down to make a turn just a little further up the road. The woman who was driving had that tint to her that almost made her seem like a ghost, and her baby in the back seat, strapped in his carrier, could have been a ghost child. But that was just the trick of the light through the windows of the car, some kind of Pontiac, I think. Playing with the child in the back seat, though, was Richard Nixon. The child was laughing as Nixon tickled him under his chin. As the car slowed down to make the turn, Nixon looked at me and gave me the victory sign. He smiled at me, his jowls sagging like they had in life, and waved his hand with two fingers raised in a vee. He was laughing, his jowls going to town. As the car turned, Nixon went back to tickling the child in the back seat.

It's not the Alzheimer's. It's no damage to brain cells that's bringing the dead to me. And I'm not crazy. I just think that, since Sarah's death, I've been lingering between living and the idea of the dead so much that the dead have been drawn to me as a kind of distraction. I mean, being dead is something it's hard to ignore, hard to get away from. And so they come to me to visit and stop thinking about being dead for a little while.

The dead aren't scary. They're more bored than anything.

Last night my best friend from my time in Korea came by. I hadn't seen Greg since that day in Korea when the mine went off and the lower half of his body turned into a red mist he looked down at, surprised. We spent hours drinking and talking about the war, about the pranks we pulled on some of the others in our outfit. He was laughing about the dead snake we put in one of the men's bunks when suddenly he went silent.

What's the matter? I asked him. Need another beer?

For a few seconds, he just looked at me. It was as if his eyes had gone suddenly blind.

Picture a room, Greg said, with shelves built in to all the walls. His eyes were closed now, and it was as if he were dreaming, his lids dancing with that rapid movement of the eyes behind them.

Now, picture the shelves are full of hearts, human hearts. But the hearts aren't quiet, Greg said, or still. They're beating, there on the shelves. Picture being surrounded by thousands of hearts beating on shelves. Imagine the music of thousands of beating hearts.

Greg, what are you talking about? I asked him.

Listen to the hearts, Greg said. I watched his eyelids jerking, and there was a faint music coming from somewhere far off. At first it was too faint to make out what song it was.

Listen, Greg said. Listen. You know this song.

The music was getting louder, more distinct. It could have been coming from the radio in the kitchen. And it did seem familiar. It got louder still, and then I knew what it was. "Moondance" by Van Morrison. One of Sarah's favorite songs. When I looked over at Greg, his eyes had stopped dancing.

In that room, Greg said, there are too many hearts. Then he got up and left.

Later, I put the CD of *Moondance* in and programmed the title track to repeat and fell asleep listening to that song. Knowing that I'd wake to the same music made it easier to fall asleep.

•　　•　　•

Tonight, on the news, there's a story about another baby being found burned. No one seems to know what's going on. The police are said to have no suspects, and according to the anchor it's been suggested there's not someone going around setting fire to babies in their cribs, that it's some kind of natural phenomenon. He says the fact there's been no evidence in any of the cases of anyone breaking in, that none of the parents have heard anything strange before they woke to find their babies dead in their cribs, and the fact that smoke detectors have not gone off, that all these things keep it from being clear just what is going on.

Can you imagine the kind of person who could do that? my mother asked. She had walked in while a reporter was interviewing the parents, who could barely talk between sobs.

Do you mean the reporter? I asked her, thinking she was disgusted, as she had often been alive, by the way reporters interview people at times that should be private, turning people's sorrow or shame or fear into a public spectacle.

No, she said, though that's despicable too. I mean a person who could set fire to a baby.

On the television, the reporter was now pointing to the house where the latest victim had been found.

I've walked by that house, I said. It was a house I'd walked past many times, just about five blocks away. I'd seen the parents out in the yard. Seen the stroller sitting nearby where they were pulling up weeds. Just a couple of nights ago, I said, the father was out watering the lawn when I went by. We said hello.

And last night, my mother said, someone walked in to that house and set fire to a baby.

Are you sure? I asked her. It's hard for me to believe, I said, that anyone could actually do that. Maybe it *is* some kind of natural phenomenon, like they said on the news.

There's nothing natural about it at all, my mother said, and went into the kitchen and was gone.

• • •

There's yellow police tape draped around some trees blocking off the yard. They won't let anyone get close to the house. It's still light out, but the sky has that look to it that says it's given up, that it's just going to get darker from here on out. Some neighbors are out working in their yards. A woman whose husband is trimming the bushes at the side of their house waves to me from where she's watering a flowerbed in the front yard. She's seen me out walking many times, and doesn't think of an old man walking by as any kind of threat, as anything dark at all.

I wave back and keep walking. This is the same block where Sarah and I stood in front of a dark house and listened to the faint sounds of lovers drifting down over us. It's just a few houses up from the house with the yellow tape running from tree to tree surrounding it. It's never the things you want to forget the Alzheimer's takes.

Like you'd want to forget anything, someone says beside me. It's my first father-in-law, Darrel. The truth of it is you'd remember everything if you could, and you know it.

Darrel and I had gotten along better than his daughter and I ever had. He had worked at the Heinz plant, too. Fact is, I met his daughter, my first wife, at a company picnic shortly after I started working at the plant. Darrel and I had fished together, even after the divorce. Fact is, I was there in the hospital room the night his bad heart finally gave out on him, after three operations. One of the last things he saw was his daughter crying in my arms.

Not everything, I say. There are some nights with your daughter I'd just as soon forget.

Yeah, Darrel says, laughing a little, but there are more you'd remember.

I have to admit he's right. But this, I say, to have to imagine someone doing this. I'd rather be able to forget it happened.

Then why are you here? Darrel asks. Why are you walking by this house tonight?

I don't know. Maybe I needed to see people still going on with their lives. Maybe I needed to see men and women who live even closer than I do to where such a thing could happen out mowing their lawns and watering flowers and cleaning windows. Maybe it's not the house where it happened I needed to see at all, but the house where Sarah and I heard two people making love. Maybe I needed to know that house is still here. Even after this.

That's a good story, Darrel says. But we both know it's not true. Gotta go, he says. Good fishing, he says, and then he's gone, and I keep walking.

The Widow as Ventriloquist
for the Past

RAY LOVED TO TALK IN VOICES. Sometimes I would rub his throat with my hands, like it was an ancient Persian vase I'd found on some beach and I was determined to let loose whatever genie had been locked away in it for centuries. I would rub his scruffy throat with my hands and call him my little macho mockingbird and coo at him as if I were some bird myself till he let one of the voices out. It was his talent.

Sometimes I would rub his throat with both hands in bed. He knew what was expected of him when I did that. He was to start talking in some famous voice and not slip out of it until we were both finished and sweaty, lying calm on top of the damp sheets. It wasn't only living voices Ray did. Sometimes the dead made love to me in the almost dark of our bedroom, the only light whatever managed to make it through the drapes of what moon there was, and the streetlamps. Jack Kennedy was my lover more than once in the seventies.

Ray couldn't say no to me, God bless his guilty heart. Ray always worried I didn't enjoy it as much as he did. Sex, I mean, not the voices. He'd do anything I asked to please me. Especially after the way things turned out with my only pregnancy, I think Ray took it upon himself, almost as a sort of burden, to do whatever it took to be sure I enjoyed sex. Pleasure being the only reason for it, after that.

Report from a Place of Burning

Sometimes Ray would let a voice out at a party. But never just for entertainment, Ray liked to say, like he was bragging. Ray said he used the voices only when to do so would teach someone a lesson they needed to learn. Ray said the voices needed to educate as well as entertain. To be used for good, Ray liked to joke, never for evil.

Like the time he did Nixon at Sam and Gloria's Independence Day backyard cook out. This was some years after the resignation but before his death and the subsequent resurrecting of his reputation. So Nixon was still just about universally an object of scorn and ridicule. Some grudges last longer than others. Ray didn't hold grudges, though, and certainly not against ousted Presidents or any other figure he knew only through the news. I can't even hold a grudge against people I love, Ray would say.

Sam and Gloria's oldest, Pamela, was thirteen at the time. The kind of thirteen which can pass, from a distance, for eighteen. With all the attendant attitude, the resentment toward any restriction placed on her, whether by her parents or by the nudges of decorum, of what people call polite society, what Ray used to laugh and, in his best Rock Hudson, call the caste of snobs. She was scowling at one end of a picnic table covered with various Tupperware containers of egg and potato salad, Jell-O with marshmallows embedded in it, deviled eggs and bags of chips of various sorts, large horseflies stirring the air just above the table and occasionally alighting on one container or another. Pamela was swatting at the flies whenever they landed. She had already had what can only be labeled a hissy fit.

I did feel for her some. I mean, she was thirteen going on grown-up and forced, on the Fourth of July, to hang out in her own backyard with a bunch of couples, her parents' friends. True, some had kids close to her age they had brought with them, but they weren't kids she hung out with. The fit was over the fact she'd been invited by some of her friends to a party out at the quarry a few miles south of town. The quarry was full of water and, unlike the quarry near the interstate, it was kept clean enough it was used as a local swimming hole. People even took scuba-diving classes there, though what they might have seen down there in that wound ripped out of the earth for some local mineral or other, I can't imagine.

That Fourth of July, like most, there were local bands playing there throughout the day and into the evening, and the promise of the biggest and best fireworks display in the county starting at dusk. Pamela took it as a personal affront that she had to wait the day out in her own back yard, surrounded by old fogies and nerds. That she had to be satisfied with the town's pathetic fireworks and a few bottle-rockets her parents wouldn't even let *her* shoot off.

Ray and I had been among the witnesses to her fit, during which she called Sam and Gloria things I would never have dared to call my parents. I might have thought them but I would never have said them. We all got to hear, too, how they treated her like a baby and how she was fed up with it. The fit came to an abrupt end when she yelled at her mother that she wished she had just died at birth. At least then, she yelled, I wouldn't have had to live long enough to be forced to spend the Fourth of July with a bunch of dweebs and losers. Gloria looked over at me with a frightened look on her face and slapped her thirteen-year-old daughter. Pamela shut up with the slap and started to cry as she turned and ran off to the picnic table farthest from her parents to pout and seethe and swat at flies and not look at her mother, no matter what.

Gloria wasn't looking at Pamela, though, or running after her. Gloria, her face still contorted as if by some fear, was looking over at me. When it hit me why she was looking at me and ignoring her daughter, looking at me with her eyes so wide, like they were pleading with me somehow, begging for forgiveness for some sort of unmentionable crime, I gave her a little smile and a nod. I could see her entire body relax from the tensing that had started up when her daughter had yelled that about wishing she'd just died at birth.

Report from a Place of Burning

And then Ray did Nixon. From the resignation speech, the one to his staff the day before he stepped up into that helicopter, stopping to wave and give his famous victory sign just before lowering his head and being swallowed by the interior darkness for the last time. What a performance, Ray had said when we watched that on TV. Ray hunched up his shoulders and loosened his jaw and cheeks so they shook a little. Not real jowls, but as close as Ray could come. Wringing his shaking hands out in front of his chest, he came out with *My mother? My mother was a saint.* I smiled and put my arms around him. All the adults, and some of the kids, broke out laughing. Gloria looked like she finally understood what it was to be truly saved. Pamela just scowled.

• • •

I don't know anymore what's wrong with this world, but I've come to expect and even to accept the worst from people. We're mad as hatters, almost every one of us. But I guess I like to believe the rest of this world, what we think of as nature, as if we were not, or are not, anymore, natural, I like to think that nature is somehow immune to our kinds of madnesses. And for a long time I was able to hold to that belief, as a kind of comfort, actually. A comfort I needed more after Ray died.

Even before that, I understood how far off some people let themselves be taken.

In his last years, Ray had taken to wanting to walk after dinner. We'd lock up the house with all the lights on and head off into the beginning of dusk. We'd vary our walks so as not to get so bored one of us couldn't make some story out of something we saw on the walk. Ray and I were good at telling stories to one another, making things mean more than they probably did.

Most of the time we'd stay in the neighborhood and wave to men and women out working on their yards, mowing the grass or trimming bushes or planting flowers. Often we would stop and

The Widow as Ventriloquist for the Past

talk with these men and women. The stories we told them were not the stories we told one another, but they were good stories and just as often made up as true. Depending on the weather, they might be watering their lawns, trying to save them from the heat. Depending on the season, we might hold onto one another waiting for a man or a teenage boy to finish shoveling the walk so we could pass on through. If no one was out, our stories started off with some figure glimpsed through a window.

Sometimes we would head downtown, which was only a matter of ten minutes or so, on foot, from our house. Even back then, walking together, we both felt, downtown, some tension around us. The poor and the desperate lived downtown. Once I heard a woman's voice asking *Where is it?* I heard this question several times before I figured out where the voice was coming from. As we passed by an old yellow brick building, one with architecture and a facing that told a story of a better past, I looked up, hearing the question again, and on the second floor a window was wide open despite the almost freezing temperature and the howling wind. This was in December. The window was open and I could see the bare, flabby arms of a woman who was old but not elderly. It was hard to tell her age for sure, but it was clear from the look on her face and her voice that this woman had seen plenty in her time. I looked around for who she was asking where it was, thinking if I saw who she was asking the meaning of the question would become clear. There was no one around, and the woman had not given any indication of seeing either of us. She kept asking where it, whatever it was, was. Ray put his hand on my arm and gave me a little push, hurrying us past the building. Ray didn't want anything to do with the woman or her question. I let him hurry me, not wanting to have to imagine the story to explain her.

On another walk, this one in warmer weather, May I think it was, Ray and I were on Main Street and in the middle of a story about a man who kept his wife and two children blindfolded. We had earlier passed the junior high and seen pairs of kids, one in each pair blindfolded and being led around the school's front lawn by the other.

The wife, blindfolded, Ray said, had learned to cook without being able to see, to set the table and wash the dishes all without being able to see what it was she was doing. His two sons had learned to throw a baseball back and forth without dropping it for hours at a time, and their games of tag were a graceful dance through the front and back yards. No one was allowed to remove the blindfolds and no one did. The man watched his blindfolded family eat and play and sleep blindfolded for many years. Since the others were blindfolded he took to leaving the lights in the house on all the time. One night he woke up in the bright light of his bedroom and knew something was wrong. There was a pain he had never felt before all through his body, Ray said.

The man who had blindfolded his family clutched at his chest and gasped a couple of times, though his wife, blindfolded and sound asleep next to him in the bed, didn't wake to the sounds of those twin scratchy gulps for air. The man who had blindfolded his family was dead, his exposed eyes rigid and staring at the light that would not go out for days yet, when the bulb, which had been on a long time and had outlived its expected life, finally gave a last short burst of almost blue light and went dark.

His blindfolded wife had given up trying to get him out of bed and down the hall, Ray said. His boys were being bad, staying up late and telling one another strange stories of sound and how it makes the air it travels through its own, throwing a Nerf ball from one bed to the other, waiting for their mother, or maybe their father, yes, maybe tonight it would be their father who would finally get out of his bed and storm down the hall to tell them to put that darn ball down and get to sleep. They hadn't heard their father for days. They didn't know what it was they'd done wrong to anger their father so. They had never known him to stay angry this long, Ray was saying, just as we passed one of the sheltered bus stops the city had placed around downtown, as if the weather there were worse than where we lived.

Through the glass smeared with god knows how many hand-prints and with weather, we saw a woman with ragged and orang-ish hair, waving her arms frantically in the air over her head. It looked like she could have been under attack from some band of itinerate and hungry insects, gnats with an attitude maybe, Ray said, or mosquitoes with acne and something sharp they swung in the air ahead of them. Nothing. There was nothing there but the woman and her ghastly hair and her arms doing their strange and jerky dance all around her head. I had no doubt Ray would change his story and he did. After we passed the woman, he started to talk about a woman gnats loved so much they couldn't leave her alone. How they loved the way her sore arms flapped around them in the humid air. Ray was already into the story, which is why he didn't see what I saw, looking back at the woman we had passed.

Her arms had stopped dancing around her head and made a sturdy and unmistakable hammock for a baby, crossed that way in front of her chest. Her head was bowed and she could have been whispering, or singing some elegant lullaby to the baby in her arms, if only her arms had not been empty. I stopped listening to the story Ray was making up as we kept walking. I didn't want to listen to any story right then. Right then, all I wanted was to go back to that woman and reach down and take the baby from her tired arms. Right then, all I wanted was to whisper the silly sounds to that baby I had never had the chance to whisper to ours. All I wanted was to make her let out one of those wonderful little baby laughs. Right then, that was all it was possible for me to even think of wanting.

•　　•　　•

I can't say what had gone wrong for that woman, no more than I can say what's gone wrong with this world. It's no doubt, though, something has. Something has very definitely gone wrong. Yester-day, on my walk, something I haven't been able to stop since Ray died, these walks, I saw the oddest thing. Three birds were flitting erratically just over the pavement and making some really ugly, disturbing sounds. As they got nearer I could see it was two crows and a pigeon. The crows were attacking the pigeon, and being rather vicious about it, too. They had the poor pigeon so rattled that it flew straight into the glass window of one of the shops on the block I was walking. It was one of those second-hand clothing shops. You know, where they dress dummies in the window in clothes so out of style that, to some folks, usually young couples, they seem trendy, original even.

The pigeon staggered on the sidewalk under the window behind which a mannequin stared off into the distance wearing a dress with so much lace it was like a thick fog wrapped tight around the stoic, feminine figure. The pigeon staggered and actually fell against the brick façade under the window. The crows landed awkward on either side of it, penning it in against the building, and started taking turns pecking at the smaller bird. There were several tufts of what looked like ragged fur on the pigeon, one on the back of its head. It was not long for this world, that pigeon. Not without help.

I turned back to the defense of the pigeon, though I have no love of pigeons. I shooed the crows away and they flew across the street, one settling on the metal arch of one of the old-fashioned street lamps the city has recently put around town, the other settling on the sill of a third floor window. Both were still eyeing the staggering pigeon. What had it done, I wondered, to deserve this? I spoke to the pigeon in a soft voice, telling it, though I had no way of knowing it was true, that it would be okay now. The crows wouldn't bother it again, I told it as gently and as soft as I could. It staggered along the sidewalk at the edge of the building and looked over at me without even the slightest hint of trust, despite my having saved it from the crows, both still perched across the street, apparently waiting to see what I would do next.

What I did was to tell the pigeon it was a pretty bird, though it wasn't, and turn and start off toward the local deli. But before

The Widow as Ventriloquist for the Past

I had gotten even twenty steps back into my walk the crows were back and pecking away at the pigeon unable to defend itself or even fly off, just stagger in a small circle and take it. I shooed the crows off again, this time with more fervor, wondering what someone driving by might think if they saw me through their palm-smeared side window, flinging my arms madly in the air and shouting something inarticulate. This time the crows flew further off than the first time, one disappearing into the sky past the buildings across the street, the other making it well down the street before it flapped down to the sidewalk. This time I didn't say anything to the poor pigeon still staggering in front of the second-hand clothing shop. What was there to say?

•   •   •

Once Ray had me straddling Charlton Heston in bed. Without my knowing it, he had grabbed the little stuffed monkey that usually sat in the rocker in the corner of the bedroom where the light from one of the windows fell in the late afternoons. With me straddling him and starting to moan, Ray reached down beside the bed and brought up Alfie, that was the monkey's name, and draped the monkey's long arms on either side of his neck as if the stuffed animal were trying to strangle him.

Get your filthy paws off me, you damn stinking ape, Charlton Heston's voice, a bit raspy but undeniably Charlton Heston, said. Laughing made me start to come and I collapsed onto Ray and Alfie and breathed in the soft odor of that fake monkey fur as my body finished its trembling.

Ray put his arms around me and, before he let Heston off for the night, said, *From my cold, dead hands.*

Ray is still so much with me sometimes it hurts so much I can't help but cry.

85

The Adulterer Fails to Balance Desire and Decorum

After the night of my confession, you might think everything was different. With me and Angela, I mean. You might think that, but you'd be wrong. Remember, this was back when I suffered under the illusion I was a moral person and confused as to just what that meant. It's not like the balance sheets I do every night after I close, or even the weekly or monthly versions.

On those balance sheets, numbers, which are much easier to understand than the simplest of people, are placed next to other numbers and there are absolutes. What's taken in must balance the value of what's gone out. And when the numbers tell me there's an imbalance somewhere in the equation, I know the tricks, the places to look for the missing numbers. I actually enjoy doing the books, and I'm good at it. Like Columbo or Monk or some other TV detective, I hunt down the variance. I have never failed to have the sheets balanced before I leave and lock up the store for the night. I like to think that's one of the reasons I was given my own store, and one of the better ones, in terms of volume, in the city, over other managers who'd put in more time as assistants than I had.

Balancing desire and decorum just isn't as cut and dried. Numbers can't, by themselves, sufficiently represent the equation. Too many shifting factors. Not to mention the whole question of context. Though it's true that my position on the question of how to determine whether or not any particular act is moral or not has shifted back and forth with enough violence almost nothing I once believed has made it through without some damage, back then the balance sheet analogy still ruled my morality, which meant I could not let that night, or any of the other nights we would walk for miles and talk about our lives, influence my behavior enough to let my hands touch her the way they were telling me they needed to. I would often walk with those hands in my pockets, just to be safe, no matter what the weather was like.

Which is not to say that things weren't different for me. Angela has admitted to a similar sort of struggle, especially after days or nights when her husband had been particularly cruel to her. When we would walk after one of those times, she has told me the way I treated her, the way I listened, really listened, to whatever she had to say, the way I made her laugh even at things she might have wanted to cry about, even the things she had, she would tell me later, been crying about earlier that evening, the way she said that being with me, walking beside me for miles, made her feel cared for, made her feel loved, all of this, she has told me, made it difficult for her not to ask me to hold her, just hold her. There came a point, of course, when she found a way to do just that, though she couched the request in such a way as to make me believe it was my decision to put my arms around her that first time. She's admitted that, too.

But back then, all I knew for sure was my own suffering. So many nights would end with me walking home alone from the old Heinz plant. That was where we parted. We would walk all around the neighborhood, just her and me and Lena, the wolf-dog, talking about our lives, our pasts, about the glimpses of people we caught through lighted windows. We would make up silly stories to explain the glimpses. And we never seemed to run out of things to say.

Once, I remember, rather early on, we had walked far enough we were pretty much out at one edge of town. We had left side-walks behind at least fifteen minutes earlier, and there were fewer and fewer street lights of any kind. We were walking alongside fields of corn and soy. The moon was full and there were only a few wisps of clouds in the sky, so the light would only dim a little now and then. With the moon, for the most part it was pretty easy to see where we were walking. And my God did she look amazing in that moonlight. She started talking about scars, saying you could learn a lot about a person by learning what scars they had and how they had gotten them.

Tell me, she said, about your scars.

So I told her. Starting with the scar behind my right ear, from when I had fallen down the basement steps and my ear had been caught on the edge of part of the railing and ripped down with enough force it ended up dangling down, the hollow of the ear pressed against the lower lobe and my neck, blood everywhere. I was only seven when this happened, I told her, and I could remember sitting on one of the steps down to the basement and holding my ear up so it was where it was supposed to be and yelling for my mother. My father was off at work somewhere. He had several jobs back then. And I couldn't yell to my brother for help. He was the one who'd been chasing me when I had fallen. I later learned he had run to get my mother as soon as he saw me fall. My mother, I told Angela, rode beside me in the cab to the hospital where some doctor or intern stitched my ear back together. I don't remember how many stitches it took, I told Angela, but I can still feel the scar behind my ear.

Can I feel it? Angela asked.

I stopped walking and bent my head down so she could feel the scar. God, her finger felt so good on that scar, and the ear her finger ran along for the length of the scar. I tried not to but I shivered as she touched it.

What other scars do you have? she asked.

Next I told her about the scar on my elbow. As I held my elbow up in the light of the full moon so she could see the paler streak of slightly raised skin that was the slash of the scar in that light, I told her how the story of this scar started a month before the night I actually got the scar. I told her how some friends of mine had convinced me to let them regress me hypnotically. One of them was really into all that past life nonsense, and had participated in several regressions with a friend of hers who was a professional psychologist. She knew what she was doing, she told me. Not only did I not believe in past lives and all, I was sure she wouldn't be able to put me under. But to humor them I said Sure, why not?

Some of what I'm going to tell you, I told Angela, is what I was told, as my memory of what happened after she set out to put me under, as they say, is not at all clear. Apparently she did put me under, and with the others helping her, she started trying to regress me, to send me back to some previous life and let me tell them who I was. For some time there was nothing. Just darkness and stars. Finally, far back, there was a snow storm and a man dressed in thick animal skins stumbling through blinding snow whipped into his face by a freezing wind. This man knew, they said I told them, that not far off in one direction or another there was a hut he had built. This man, I told Angela, knew his family was there, gathered around a fire. Some of them, he hoped, were thinking of him. This man also knew he was dying, that he would not make it back to that hut, that fire, those other bodies. This man had collapsed in the storm and was freezing to death.

When my friend tried to bring me out of this, bring me forward, as it were, I, or the man, or someone, refused. My friend tried a couple of different times to bring me back, but I, or whoever it was, kept refusing. Later my friend said it wasn't me who was refusing to come back. She said it was the man dying in the snow. He didn't want to be left alone, she said.

So my friend ended up calling the psychologist, who came and helped get me out. After which he spent some time with her off in another room. We could tell by the tone of his voice he was not happy with her. When she came back in after seeing him out none of us were sure whether the tears on her face were from concern for me or from being chewed out by the psychologist. She didn't try any more regressions on her own, though.

So how did you get the scar? Angela asked, tracing the scar on my elbow with her finger. I shivered, lowered my elbow, and stuck my hands in my pockets.

A month later, I told her, I was on a camping trip with my best friend. You have to understand, I said, what kind of camping trip this was. This was the kind of camping trip where, right after you set up your tent you open the cooler and start drinking, and you don't stop drinking till you're both so exhausted you have to sleep. You drink and walk around and talk yourselves into exhaustion. That kind of camping trip.

We had finished drinking for the first night, just after some rain had forced us into the tent. We had both gone to sleep pretty quickly, I told her. Apparently, I said, I woke up having to answer the call of nature, as they say. We had set up camp near the ridge of a fairly deep gully. I must have headed back to the gully to take care of business. Some time later, my friend woke up and realized I was not in the tent. He waited a while, he told me later, I said, and when I didn't come back he went out looking for me.

It was still drizzling. He said he heard something which led him over to the gully and when he looked down he saw me lying about forty or fifty feet down the side of the gully. I must have slipped and fallen along the side of the gully until gravity wore out or something stopped my fall. My friend said he freaked out. He thought I was dead, or at the very least dying. He scuffed his way down the side of that gully, managing to stay on his feet somehow until he got to where I was lying.

Now here's the strange part, or part of the strange part, of the story, I told Angela. My friend swears this is true. I don't remember any of this. This is all from him, what he told me the next morning. He said he tried to get me up to help me back up to the tent, and I told him not to touch me. The thing is, though, he swore it wasn't my voice. He said I told him not to touch me in someone else's voice. He said it didn't sound anything like me at all. He said he tried again to get me up. This time, in this voice that was not my voice, I told him that if he touched me again I, or whoever it was who was speaking, would kill him. My friend said he didn't know what to do. He couldn't just leave me down there alone at the bottom of a gully in the rain, but he was afraid to touch me. So he sat down beside me and waited.

He said that for the next twenty minutes or so he waited next to me while I made other sounds, inarticulate, even inhuman sounds, he said. Finally, he said, he noticed my body go calm and he asked if I was alright and I answered him in my own voice and let him help me back up to the tent. I had twisted my ankle and had some cuts along my back, but the worst was the gash on my elbow. The scar is all that remains of that night in the gully.

Who do you suppose was talking? Angela asked.

That's the other strange part of this story, I told her. Later I learned that the friend who had tried to regress me was telling the story of that regression and the problems in getting me back from it to some people at the very time I was falling down into that gully and lying there and threatening my friend in someone else's voice.

Ooh, she said. That is strange. Eerie.

I didn't tell her about my other scar. The one from the only operation I had ever had. She would find that scar herself, later, and I would tell her then how one of the only clear memories I have of my childhood is of being left in a hospital corridor on a bed they had wheeled off to the side after having wheeled me from my room where I'd been given a shot that was supposed to put me to sleep. I was waiting to be wheeled into surgery, I sort of knew that. And I knew I was supposed to be going to sleep. But I was not going to sleep. I was lying there awake and looking around at other people, children and adults, lying on other beds that lined either side of the corridor. I remember panicking because they were all asleep. I was the only one awake. I remember a woman with a mask over her face coming over and looking at my face and saying, muffled, that I was ready. He's out, I remember her saying. And though I wanted to tell her I wasn't out, that I was still awake and that they couldn't start the operation with me still awake, though I wanted to say something to let them know she was wrong, I couldn't make my mouth move. I remember being wheeled past opening doors and then I was out.

Angela, when I asked, said she didn't have any scars. I guess that should have told me something.

•   •   •

Sometimes it's odd the things you remember. Just a few months ago, we were at the end of one of our walks and were sipping Bailey's from a flask I had taken to carrying. We were in one of the buildings in better condition of the old Heinz plant. We had found a number of chairs in the rubble and had cleared out a space with some desks in pretty good shape. We often ended our walks there. We were sipping Bailey's and Angela had straddled my lap so that, when she wasn't sipping from the flask, she had her arms around my neck and her inner thighs pressed up against my outer thighs. The morality argument had changed by this time.

There we were, holding each other in this burnt-out shell, this place a fire had flashed through, and, while Lena was chasing some sort of insect, jumping and trying to close her mouth around it in midair, Angela was talking about her fears over having a child. Her husband had done such a number on her by that time. She was convinced she was worthless.

I think you'd make a great mother, I told her. I'd love to have a child with you.

I said this into her hair, as she was pressed up against me, her head on my shoulder, her arms around me and my hands on her back, rubbing her back like I often did.

No one's ever said that to me, she whispered. It almost sounded like she was trying to keep from crying. I held her tighter. Later, I thought, I would tell her how I had never felt the desire to have a child before in my life. But with her I wanted a child. I didn't tell her that then. It just didn't seem right, not in that ashen place.

I never did find the time or the place to tell her, and now, of course, I wish I had told her that night. Now that she's pregnant. With his child.

•   •   •

Things are different. I can't even watch bad TV without crying. Even some stupid, insipid half hour situation comedy. If something works out for some couple, if they go through some silly trial in the first sixteen minutes and in the last seven work things out and they hug one another, I can't stop crying. I keep tissues by the chair I sit in to watch TV to dry the tears. I cry with hour-long dramas and movies and anything where two people struggle through some dilemma and make things work out. I cry because I know what a lie that is. I cry for all I have lost. I cry at home in front of the TV.

Angela's given her two weeks' notice.

Tonight I cried with the local news. There was no way not to. They found another baby charred and dead in its crib. Again, like the others, nothing else in the room burned, and the parents never heard anything, no crying of the baby as it started to burn, no wailing of the fire alarm on the wall almost right next to the crib, no sounds of broken glass or forced entry. Nothing. Like all the others. The police have no suspects, the reporter said. She wasn't smiling. Sometimes a certain amount of decorum is required.

What is going on? I can't stop crying. All over town, babies are going off, like little Molotov cocktails, in their cribs. Seven of them so far, and counting. And Angela is carrying his child. I can't stop crying long enough to curse God. I need to stop crying. I need to curse God.

The Mother Gets Back Her Tragic Intuition

I WAS THE FIRST to be able to say what had happened, how it had started, at the Heinz plant. The fire that gutted so much of it and closed it down.

Arson was the suspicion. It's what we started with, the assumption someone had been pissed off enough to set fire to the plant. Heinz, of course, didn't want it to be arson. They needed the report to read *accident* so they could just write off the plant as a loss and save a bundle on taxes.

For days my team and I made our way from one part of the plant to another, while outside the chain-link fence the men and women who had worked at the plant milled about, even those who had been on shift when the fire started and had had to file out through the smoke and the blaring of the alarms and the almost-recognizable-as-human voice booming over the alarm telling everyone to *Leave the building immediately.* Some looked as if they hadn't slept since that panicked waltz through the smoke and the sirens. Some held babies or the hands of small children dancing beside them. Some held onto the fence as they watched us moving among the still-smoking ruin of the plant with our notebooks and our tape recorders and our video cameras. They were all waiting to learn what would happen to them.

I couldn't tell them anything. Certainly not anything they

needed to hear. What Heinz would decide to do wasn't what I was there for. I was there looking for the cause. I was there to trace the fire back to its beginning and there to find either motive or faulty equipment, malice or random chance.

This was not the first time I'd been in charge. I had come up fast in the company. Seems I had a flair for the work, an intuitive grasp of details in and around tragic events that helped me to focus the attention of others in ways that almost always bore fruit. Guess you could say I was a bit of a phenom. And my team knew it. They had already, by the Heinz plant fire, come to trust my intuition, even more than I did.

The suspicion was arson, but my intuition was telling me something else. We combed each of the buildings the fire had gutted while men and women suddenly left without jobs made an event out of watching us. They picnicked on the lawn just outside the chain-link fence their children would climb on till they yelled at them to get down off that fence and come over and eat their egg or tuna salad sandwiches. Outside that fence was the feel of a festival mixed with the scent of desperation. Children of varying ages were running around loudly engaged in games my intuition had no feel for, and their parents stood at the fence or sat on the lawn facing the fence and their eyes stayed focused on my team with an almost religious fervor.

It was on the third day I noticed it. It's possible several of us had gone right by it more than once without thinking a thing of it. Maybe it was because that day was clouded over and threatening rain. Maybe it was the almost greenish tinge to the light that made it through the clouds, a light someone remarked meant it was tornado weather. Maybe it was just random chance. Whatever it was, we still had an audience, despite the threat of rain, and they knew something was up. Those loitering on the lawn got up and came to the fence to peer through it. Something's about to happen, they must have been muttering among themselves. Something had been discovered.

Report from a Place of Burning

I called Gene over right off. He had the video camera. I wanted him to record what we saw as I started to pull some of the collapsed wall away. I called Ralph over to help with the bigger chunks of fallen wall. The watchers outside the fence were pointing to where the three of us were working together. They must have been asking one another what this meant, what was happening. Some must have been calculating what part of the plant the three of us were rooting about in.

Once we'd gotten enough of the charred rubble cleared away, it was obvious to each of us what we had found. Beth and Carl joined us without my even having to call for them. They had figured something was up and headed over.

Well, Gene said, guess it wasn't arson after all.

Nope, I said. Too bad, I said and smiled. We all chuckled a little and set to work recording every detail for our report.

Only the children past the fence ignored us, playing some game that required them to run for a bit before diving into the grass and rolling as if they were on fire and trying to put it out, rolling over and over and getting up and running again before they dove and repeated the roll. All the out-of-work adults were watching us, as if nothing could be happening to their kids that could come close to what it was we were doing.

• • •

Where's my intuition now? Where was it the night Samuel needed it to kick in and wake me and send me in to him while he could still be saved?

Last night I dreamt I was back working. Gene and Beth and Carl and Ralph were with me, moving through a room that had no apparent damage, though there was a heavy odor of smoke in the air. The room seemed familiar, but something about it was off.

The dimensions, I said. The dimensions aren't right.

I told Beth to get some measurements, to make them accurate. She started sticking pins in the walls at regular intervals but everything kept shifting until the pins were not regular in their spacing at all. In fact, it began to look like the pins Beth was sticking in the walls were taking on a shape, some sort of four-legged animal. And whatever it was, it was running in an awkward motion, like in a very old movie. A jerky motion. The room began to take on the grainy quality of those old movies. All around us, unrecognizable animals were panicking and trying to run off.

I can't get these measurements right, Beth said, almost in tears. They're fighting me.

Forget it, I said. It's not important.

Carl put his arms around Beth to comfort her. Nothing about any of this was right, I knew. Still, it all felt so familiar. Where had I seen Carl put his arms around Beth like that?

Over here, Gene said from behind the glare of the light on his camera. He was taping something. The odor of smoke and of something else got stronger as the rest of us moved toward the light. Suddenly the stench of smoke and the other was too much and I was choking. Gene was standing over a crib and pointing the camera down into it, but there was no baby in the crib. Instead, there was a ruptured pipe. Light from the camera was in my eyes, and I couldn't make out what the pipe was.

Then a baby was crying in the crib.

Samuel, I whispered. What's wrong, Samuel? I reached into the crib to lift my baby out of the dark and smoky place and my arms were burning. The flames of my arms touched Samuel and set him on fire and both of us were burning in that room that was suddenly smaller, too small for all of us. Of course, no one but Samuel and I were there, both of us on fire. I picked up my burning baby and held him to my breast, and the room was nothing but fire.

I woke up sweating and tangled in the sheets, alone in the bed. Harlan was sleeping in the living room on the couch, as he had taken to doing when I would get too violent in my sleep. I could hear his gentle snoring.

The monitor was silent. It was still hooked up to the other monitor in what had been Samuel's room, but both had been turned off since that night. Harlan had wanted to put the monitors away in a closet somewhere, but I said no. Some nights when I wake up at three in the morning, a habit I haven't been able to break myself of yet, I imagine I hear Samuel's little sleep-noises coming out of the speaker. Some nights I can swear I hear his little body shifting, asleep.

Some nights, I want to tell Harlan but haven't yet, Samuel's ghost drifts into the monitor. Those are the nights I hear the quiet shifting of what used to be his body under the blankets I had wrapped around him in his crib after singing him to sleep.

Some days, I hear those little sounds he used to make that I said were him giggling. It makes me feel a little better for a while, thinking that Samuel is off playing somewhere, able to laugh and more. There are times when I hear those little noises he would make when he was at my breast. When I hear those sounds my breasts ooze milk still. There's so much I don't understand anymore.

• • •

Harlan doesn't think what I'm painting is good for me. I'm not sure, Honey, it's healthy, he says.

Fires are everywhere. Canvases of all sizes surround me. Some are hung on the walls, some are on easels, and others, on the floor, lean against the walls. Over twenty different canvases in various stages, and on each of them a fire. Some have what look to be structures of some kind, as if the fire's wrapped around what's left of a house or a factory. There are places where blackened wood beams are almost plainly visible. In other canvases, shattered glass and melting plastic window-frames give in to flames.

My current favorite canvas is a large one, eight feet by ten feet. Visible amidst the burning on this one is a wall in which a number of pins have been stuck. The pins, done with excruciating detail, are beginning to melt. Some are dripping green or blue or red plastic onto what must have been a floor. The metal interiors of the pins will stay, and are staying, embedded in the wall, which

The Mother Gets Back Her Tragic Intuition

is charring and breaking out here and there into flames that will finally consume everything in the canvas, of this I have no doubt. But for now there is a kind of stasis suggested by what remains of those melting pins.

And the pattern of charring along the wall should tell me something about how this fire started. If I had my intuition still I could say what that is. I could probably say how this fire had started. I'm sure I could. I should be able to. It's tearing me up that I can't say what it is I should know from this. All I can do now is paint the fire and the damage it does. There's very little I can say about it. Maybe Harlan is right. Maybe what I'm painting isn't healthy.

* * *

When the wrens and the sparrows aren't enough, with their little songs, to keep me in bed sobbing all day, I paint. When I'm not painting and not in bed crying, I spend time working on my scrapbook. Harlan has seen the scrapbook only once, close to when I started keeping it. He found it on the kitchen table where I had left it for a moment while I hunted down some scissors, and he opened it to see what it was. When he saw what was in it, Harlan started to cry, standing there in the kitchen holding the open scrapbook. I waited till he put it back on the table and went out the back door before coming back to it with the scissors to add another article from the newspaper.

The scrapbook is a little history of sorts. A history of this season of burning babies. I have cut and pasted all the articles I could find in the local paper, all the grainy photographs. None of the photographs are clear and most are so dark it's impossible to say what the photograph's of, not without the help of the captions, which say things like The body of Aaron Finter, found by his parents smoldering in his crib the morning of the 15th.

Nothing's explained in this scrapbook. Everything is speculation, theory after theory proposed and shot down by a whole host of experts. Reconciliation is not what this scrapbook is about. I can't imagine reconciliation is even possible in this world anymore.

Report from a Place of Burning

I think that's what worries Harlan the most. Harlan still works, still goes out into the world most days and talks to people because he has to. Some he talks to because they are friends and offer him some solace with their company. Because he goes out into the world almost every day and has these conversations, he has, he has said to me, a sense of the passing of time.

Distance, he says to me, it's distance you need. Not the fire over and over again, stilled in time in those canvases.

Harlan has it wrong. Nothing is stilled in the canvases. It all rages on, a fury of motion and consummation. Nothing is still. Nothing.

The Detective Gives Up on Coincidence

NOT ENOUGH SLEEP makes the world move in ways that just aren't right. The body knows this but the brain, reeling from lack of oxygen, keeps arguing, positing new theories of space and time to explain the wrong motion. DeGreco says exhaustion is the body's way of either getting something done so it can rest or, if that doesn't happen, at least making things interesting.

The photos I've taken of all seven of the charred babies are pinned up around our office. Every one of the seven, in those cribs, looks like some genetic experiment gone awry, with what's left of their tiny arms crossed over their chests. The last few days, when I haven't been out interviewing folks connected to the case, I've been in this office reading lab reports, going over them for something, some clue we keep missing. It's got to be there. DeGreco's right about that, though not even DeGreco, not even the legend, has been able to see it yet. Hours I'm at this cluttered desk, scanning reports which sound the same, the seven dead babies watching me from the walls of the office, from the photographs I took of them smoldering in their cribs. It's no wonder I haven't slept.

• • •

Yesterday I was back at the scene of the fifth victim. It was the husband, Harlan, who came to the door and it was Harlan I was there

101

to talk to, due to a caller who wondered if he was doing the right thing, calling the police.

I don't want to cause trouble for no one, especially someone who recently lost a baby that way, the man said.

Just what is it that's on your mind, sir? I asked. Patience, DeGreco says, comes in handy when you've got some time to kill. That DeGreco, what a card.

Well, I work with Harlan Burke. A while ago, his baby, Samuel, burned in his crib, like the others. You know?

Yes, sir. I'm one of the detectives assigned to the case. I've met Mr. Burke and his wife.

It's really about his wife, detective. The other day Harlan seemed worse and when I asked if there was anything I could do, he asked me to tell him if I thought it was strange, what his wife was doing, and he told me about how she'd taken up painting again, since the death of Samuel, something she hadn't done since college. I told him I didn't think that was strange. She needs something to fill up her time, I told him. Sounds perfectly natural.

Not the painting, he said. That I could deal with, even see it as a good thing. It's what she spends her time painting that gets to me.

What does she paint? I said, to remind him he hadn't actually told me yet, since it seemed he thought he had.

Fires, he told me. She paints fires. She's got over a couple dozen canvases of different sizes all going, all of fires. In some, he told me, it looks like some building is burning, you can see some beams and maybe part of a wall here and there. In others it looks like there might be animals running in the flames, he said, animals on fire themselves and frantic.

I've never seen Harlan look so haunted. I wasn't sure I should call, but I told my wife and she said the police might want to know.

I thanked him and assured him he'd done the right thing in calling me, though I still can't really say that's true. It was odd enough, though, I felt I had to look into it. DeGreco agreed but left me to do it on my own. It was a test, I knew that. So I did some background on Harlan's wife and found out that her team had been the one sent in by the insurance company to determine the cause of the Heinz plant fire a couple of years ago. That it wasn't long after that she announced her pregnancy and requested a leave of absence. Now, her child's the fifth victim in this hideous killing spree and she's painting fires. Could of course just be coincidence. DeGreco says he doesn't believe in coincidence.

Coincidence, DeGreco says, is the world's way of rubbing our noses in it. Whatever *it* may be, he adds.

It warranted a visit, that's for sure, and DeGreco said I should handle this one solo. On my way out to the Burke place, I decided I should speak to the husband about this first, alone. Get as much ammunition as I can before taking her on, was my thinking.

Mr. Burke, I said when he opened the door. You might remember me. I was here a couple of weeks ago, with Detective DeGreco. About your son? I didn't want to have to say anything else to remind him.

Of course, detective. What can I do for you? It was creepy, the way his face didn't seem to have any actual expression to it. How it didn't change, not one muscle, not one subtle inflection of motion.

I just have some follow-up questions, if you have a few minutes?

He invited me in and we sat down in the living room, me in the chair where his wife sat with those burned arms held as though she were still holding onto the smoldering ruin of her child. Harlan found it hard to look directly at me sitting in that chair, which was fine by me. I asked if his wife was at home and he looked back towards the nursery and said she was, that she was working.

Should I get her? Harlan said.

No. Actually, sir, I wanted to talk to you first. He nodded, relaxed that he would not have to go back to that room where she was painting to get her. It's come to our attention, Mr. Burke, that you may be concerned about how your wife is handling the loss of your son. I didn't know how else to start this. Whatever I said was bound to be awkward, and likely to hit some nerves that no doubt were still awful raw. Bull's eye, DeGreco, if he'd been there, would have said and smiled that odd smile of his, the one that isn't really a smile.

What are you talking about?

One of your colleagues at work has told us you're worried about what your wife's been painting since Samuel's death. That got the face to change. What it changed to wasn't what I'd have expected, though. Harlan Burke looked afraid. Scared to death, actually.

Someone told you about the paintings? he said. It was clear he was trying hard not to look down the hall toward the nursery.

Yes sir, I said. I didn't push it. I needed to watch what Harlan came to on his own, if anything. How he got to it, whatever it was, would tell me what I needed to know. I'd been working with De-Greco long enough to know that.

What is it, exactly, Harlan, you're afraid of? Bring it to the personal level, first names, and name it, the fear, what it was, was my thinking.

What are you saying? he said. You can't think, and he couldn't get the rest out.

I'm not accusing you or your wife of anything, Harlan. Believe me. It was clear he didn't.

Look, Harlan said, his face really something now, a muddle of different expressions, none of them matching what was coming out of his mouth, except maybe the undertone of anger, so she spends her time painting nothing but fires consuming buildings and animals and yes, maybe people. That doesn't mean, and again he couldn't say it out loud.

Calm down, Mr. Burke. A little distance, a bit of formality, I'd decided, was what was called for. I'm not saying I think your wife is capable of setting a baby on fire, much less her own. But you must admit, sir, it's strange, her painting all these fires.

Harlan had turned at a noise in the hall, his wife going to the bathroom. Come here, he said. Come with me. I followed Harlan

The Detective Gives Up on Coincidence

down the hall to the room I had taken so many pictures of. The crib was nowhere in sight. Probably put away in the attic, I thought. This was no nursery anymore. Canvases were strewn around the room, more than twenty of them, and each had at least the beginnings of flames. This room that hadn't been touched by the fire that had taken their son was now consumed by fire, the fire this mother was condemning the room to.

That's how I saw it, and that's what I would tell DeGreco later. She's not the one, I'd say. Those fires she's painting, it's both a kind of revenge and a kind of survivor guilt. That room, the room she's painting in, the room that used to be a nursery, she's angry at it. Why, she yells through the paintings, why didn't you burn with my son? You should have burned, the paintings scream. And she sits in the midst of these canvases of flame painting more fire, fire enough to consume her as well.

She's painting those fires to surround herself with a physical manifestation of her own hell, is what I would tell DeGreco later.

Not bad, DeGreco would say. You're catching on.

But I had to deal with Harlan Burke first. I put my arm on his shoulder and led him back out to the living room. He was collapsing, inside, I could tell. Harlan was a wreck.

You've got to let her work this out, Harlan. Remember that in the Bible, Harlan, the Holy Spirit is a flame. Fire, the Bible tells us, can purify without consuming. It can refine. Think of the fires she's painting as purifying fires, cleansing fires. I assured him we'd keep at it till we found whoever killed their son, and the others, and shook his hand before showing myself out, leaving Harlan sitting with his face in his hands in the chair where his wife had tried to hold on to the ghost of their son.

• • •

I'm not sure what's worse. Facing people whose lives have been ruined by this bastard burning up babies, or staying in the office looking over lab reports and being watched over by all seven of the burned babies in the glossy eight by tens pinned to the walls. I can't say for sure whether the silence of the babies is easier or harder to take than the noise the survivors make out of their anger and their pain and their fear.

Death is a mute, I heard DeGreco tell an officer once, whose hands have been chopped off at the wrists.

• • •

This afternoon it was an old guy whose wife died years ago. He was pretty far down the list, but we've got nothing, no leads, and we're desperate. Some of the neighbors said this old guy was a regular. He must walk, one said, for exercise. A woman told me he used to walk with a younger woman they had figured out, finally, was his wife, but she had died some time ago. Everyone said that, since he regularly walked the neighborhood, he might have seen something that, put into context, just might help nail the sicko setting fires to babies in their cribs. Or maybe, one woman said, a woman no one else talked to, a woman one of the other neighbors had suggested might be worth looking at for it, maybe that old guy is the one who's doing it.

I waited where several said he'd be by soon and, sure enough, before too long here comes this old guy obviously in pretty good shape for his age. He fit the description the neighbors had given me. At one point, when he was still several hundred feet off, I could've sworn he was talking to someone, though no one was there. He wasn't just talking with this person who wasn't there, they were arguing. The old guy was using his arms and, whatever the argument was about, I could tell something about the guy I'm sure DeGreco would've noticed, too. He was pretending he was absolutely certain about whatever it was he was saying. He wanted to be certain, maybe needed to be, but he wasn't sure at all. In fact, he was scared he was wrong.

Excuse me, sir, I said, holding out my badge, which caught the sun and almost blinded the old guy. I was wondering if you'd mind if I asked you a few questions.

The Detective Gives Up on Coincidence

No problem, son, he said.

I've been told you walk through this neighborhood pretty regularly.

It's for my health mainly, though it's a nice area to walk through. Some really beautiful older Victorian homes, he said, and the people here have their lawns landscaped nicely.

I was told you walked by the house where a baby was found dead several days ago. I heard you walked by that night, and were seen stopped at the house, by the yellow police tape.

What kind of man or woman could do such a sick thing, burn a baby, and do it over and over? The way he shook his head, there was sadness in it, sure, but there was wisdom, too. Even without DeGreco's help, I could tell this guy was not involved. This guy knew guilt intimately and, despite the act he put on for the people he chatted with as he strolled past their homes, he had, as they say, a dark side. He had something to hide, but it wasn't the murder of seven babies burned in their cribs. It was something more personal, more intimate. Something I knew I'd never get him to admit.

I wish I could tell you, sir, I said. I asked if he had noticed anything unusual in the days leading up to the child's death. I could tell there was something.

Can't think of anything, officer. Sorry, he said.

Again, I knew whatever it was he had seen had nothing to do with what was happening to the babies, but that he had seen something odd. Something so odd he was afraid to admit it, afraid what it would say about him if he did.

Another dead end, I knew, and watched him walk off at a good clip for such an old guy. Just before he turned the corner and headed south, he said something. I could see his face from the side and he was talking to someone, but there was nobody there. Great, I thought. The guy hears voices. Still, he wasn't our guy, and I was sure of that. Leave him alone, I thought, to talk to whoever it is he thinks he's talking to.

Report from a Place of Burning

Talking is always a good thing, DeGreco says, even if no one's listening.

Maybe, DeGreco. Maybe especially when no one is listening. Maybe the man who can go on talking when there's no longer any reason to do so is the sanest one of us all.

Or maybe I'm just trying to justify my singing lullabies when DeGreco is out of the office and it's just me and the seven dead babies hung on the walls in their charred and smoldering final poses. It's not really the babies I'm soothing with the singing. I don't believe in ghosts. What haunts me isn't the tiny spirits of the seven murdered babies, but the lack of evidence. What haunts me is that we still don't know how these babies are being burned the way they are, why they're being burned, or who it is burning them. We don't have a clue, and that haunts me. No lullaby is going to change that, I know.

•　　•　　•

DeGreco called and left a message while I was out. Said he may have a lead, that we may have gotten the break we've been looking for. Said that we needed to speak to a prophet.

I wanted to laugh at that. A prophet. Maybe it was the seven babies pinned up around the office, or maybe it was remembering how that old guy argued with someone who wasn't there, but whatever it was I couldn't laugh. Maybe faith, I thought, isn't a bad direction to look in. Maybe, I said to no one at all as I turned out the light and left the babies in the dark, this prophet can tell us some things.

The Prophet and the Gorge

AND THE DRAGON STOOD before the woman which was ready to be delivered, St. John wrote, for to devour her child as soon as it was born.

Even modern medicine can't deny the dragon its meal every time. The dragon, it will eat and know the fullness of wriggling life in its maw. Fire is the breath of this dragon which does not consume the flesh but the spirit.

The local news is abuzz with reports of babies burned and dead in their cribs. People are talking everywhere I go about these babies, but no one is talking dragons.

Signs are signs despite blindness.

•　　•　　•

The gorge we played in and around as kids, despite the gorge where it was legal to swim being just a mile or two away, holds more than the fiery body of the diver in its murky water. They dragged the gorge for his body but all the hooks ever brought up out of that brackish water was a red hand, torn from the arm at the wrist. The rest of that red diver is a mystery.

I was the last to see it. Tied to a fence, I watched that body, which plummeted like some fanatical star off a bridge to collapse against stone and slide gracefully under what water there was in the gorge. It was lower than usual due to a drought, one reason why no one could figure how the hooks could have missed the body.

I refused to swim in the gorge that summer. My brother and others, Jack and Ted included, would come back from taking a swim in those illegal waters, their bodies already beginning to break out in the rash that would take days and at least half a bottle of calamine lotion to get rid of, and they would tell me stories of their encounters with the red diver.

He's alive, my brother would start.

Yeah, alive and swimming around down at the bottom of the gorge, Ted took up the story. That's why they didn't find him when they dragged the gorge.

That's right, Jack chimed in. He ripped his own hand off and stabbed it onto the hook so they would go away and leave him alone. The one he has left, Jack said, is webbed now, just like his feet. I saw them, up close, he said. Between the fingers and all the toes he's grown flaps of skin he can stretch taut. They help him swim, he said.

Not only that, my brother said. He's got gills. I saw them, swear I did. Along his torso, where you can sometimes see the shadows of the ribs under the skin and muscle, that's where the gills are. Pink slashes in his red sides. I was close enough to see them move and bubbles were let go from inside those gills, from inside his body.

I doubt he even uses his lungs, Jack said.

Sure he does, Ted said. When he climbs out of the water and claws his way up one of the sides of the gorge to come out and walk around town at night when people are sleeping. They say he's looking for his lost hand, Ted said. They say he wheezes from his wet lungs and whimpers his way through town, looking.

They would tell different versions of these stories. Sometimes as cautionary tales. Behave or the red diver will come for you, that sort of thing. Sometimes they were just variations on horror stories, the red diver just a figure of mindless fear, an indiscriminate killer, especially of little boys. Once or twice the red diver became

The Prophet and the Gorge

a sort of angel sent down to bless and swim the holy waters of the gorge, and the only ones who could see him swimming through the green water were the consecrated.

Seeing the red diver, in these stories, was a good sign. Swimming by the red diver without touching was good for calming the heart, they said. And to be touched by the one remaining red hand was a blessing.

Local myths don't ask any less for faith just because they're local.

Over the next few years, stories of the red diver were told less and less, though those that were told became more and more detailed, more and more believable despite being outrageous. The red diver took on more of a personality in these later stories, and worked his magic more one on one. And, of course, as with almost any local legend, there were miracles associated with the red diver.

Like the boy, I think he was related to Ted in some way, who had an epileptic fit sunning on one of the flat rocks of the gorge and rolled off the rock into the stinking water. Ted watched him go under and dove from another rock down into the foul pond. When he came back up a minute later, gasping and spitting out water, his arms were wrapped around the pale body of what was his cousin, I think. They say he's never had another fit. They say the doctors can find no evidence the boy ever had epilepsy. It's a miracle, they say. It's as if the boy who slipped off that rock into the water died that day and a new boy, fixed and whole, was dragged out by his cousin and had the water forced out of his lungs so hard his ribs would ache for days.

Then there were the stories of women who woke up in the wee hours of the morning and found themselves walking towards the gorge. Sleepwalking, they were. That was the explanation the doctors gave it. The women would wake up outside in their pajamas or nighties. It's said those who didn't wake up would walk all the way out to the gorge and lay down on one of the flat rocks around the water in the gorge. It's said the red diver would crawl out of the water and sit beside them looking down at their faces and undo the nighties and slip off the pajamas and have his way with the women right there on the rocks under a full moon.

Just the other day I heard someone say that maybe the babies burning up around town had been spawned by the red diver. The red diver, a man in the grocery store said to his wife, he's been busy again. It's his offspring that are going up in flames. His wife hushed him and looked around to make sure no one else had heard what her husband had said to her.

Don't say things like that, she said. That's just awful.

And it *was* an awful thing to say. Especially if it's true.

Woe to the inhabitants of the earth and of the sea, St. John wrote, for the devil is come down unto you, having great wrath, because he knoweth that he hath but a short time.

•   •   •

The gorge holds other signs. The gorge is a place of miracles, a place of revelations. It was two years before I was able to swim in the gorge's murky waters. By then I had begun to think of the red diver, whoever or whatever he had been in the beginning, as a kindly figure, almost a sort of protector. He had become so familiar, what with all the different stories told about him, that he seemed family. I still had not read St. John's Revelation and was years away from understanding what the red diver had really been, and who he had dove into that vile water for.

Even though I only half-believed the stories my brother and his friends told, I expected to bump into his rotting body. Of course the red diver made no appearance while I swam. It was a warm day, and the water in the gorge was lukewarm. It's better swimming when the water's still cool, but it was wet and I was swimming and there were no bodies floating in my way and that was good enough.

I'd been in the water swimming for probably twenty minutes or so when I got a little dizzy. I stopped swimming and just kicked my legs and waved my arms enough to keep me afloat while I shook my head. I remember thinking it might be heat stroke, but it wasn't that hot and I hadn't been out that long, I knew. I shook my head again and started to swim.

I was almost sure I heard it, a voice as the sound of many waters, just as St. John wrote. If it was a voice, it was not speaking English, of that I was certain. I could make out only two words, floating and shaking my head and listening there in the rancid waters of the gorge.

Alpha and Omega.

I did not know then the meaning of what it was I was being allowed to hear. It would be years before I would come to understand the significance of those two words. But they came to me, Alpha and Omega, that day through the green waters of the gorge, the green waters that held not only my body moving through that stillness but somewhere the handless but otherwise perfectly preserved body of the red diver.

• • •

And there arose a smoke out of the pit, St. John wrote, as the smoke of a great furnace; and the sun and the air were darkened by reason of the smoke of the pit.

The gorge, I have come to understand, is a local manifestation of the pit. This is why it has been a place of signs for me. This is why I still duck through where the fence was cut long ago and never mended to climb down to the brackish water and slide my naked body in to swim. Why after swimming in that water the tattoo on my thigh burns and lifts from the flesh around it.

Whether the children burned in their cribs are the offspring of the red diver, or whether they are signs in their own right I do not know. Signs, when we are too close to them, are often hard to read. But one thing is clear.

This world is more and more one of fury, of rage. This world more and more is caught in so much motion it can't even pretend to stop. And with such motion much is lost. With such motion, perspective becomes a blur. How can we say where we are when where we are is in constant motion? How can we say what is when all that is is ever in flux?

Such is the dilemma of this modern world, and the curse of all of us who must live through these times. Whether we be prophets or blind men. There are some blindnesses we all must suffer with.

Though I have had a vision, blurred though it may be. A vision of angels leaping from invisible bridges in the skies and diving into the pits that open under us every day, though we do not see them, the angels or the pits. In this vision, the angels are on fire as they head for the pits open below us.

And the stars of heaven fell unto the earth, St. John wrote.

In this vision, these angels of flame pass through those most recently come to flesh among us and leave the small bodies charred and still behind them, and the pits swallow up these falling fires.

And in this vision the charred bodies left behind by the flaming dives of the angels begin to make a sound. A hum it is, but not as if a tune is being hummed. No, this hum is an insect hum, and with each charred body the hum grows louder.

And there came out of the smoke, St. John wrote, locusts upon the earth.

This insect hum is the whirring of a host of locusts, gathering and waiting to plunge into this world out of these charred remains. What the locusts will be hungry for is the flesh of those who don't believe. A terrible consummation is coming.

And no matter what horse I may sit upon and no matter what names I may read in white stones, I cannot stop what comes.

The Widower and Dali's Burning Giraffe

SOMETIMES WHEN THE DEAD COME TO ME, they're coughing or seem to have other signs of some sort of illness. A sick ghost? was my thought the first time it happened. What in the world do you do for a sick ghost? Can you press a cold wash cloth to his or her head to break the fever? Without a body, how do you check a ghost for fever? Really all you can do is to try to make them comfortable. The dead have to heal themselves, and to hear them bitch about it you'd think nothing could be more unfair.

Sometimes the dead can't complain. Babies, for instance. When the dead died as babies they can't bitch about it, since, in their bodies, they never learned language. The charred babies who have been put into the earth the last few months have nothing to say to me when they do show up, one or two waddling from the bathroom to the upstairs guest room, or all of them, gathered around my bed and holding hands and swaying to the sound of someone, maybe some Pope, chanting something in Latin. Sometimes I try to make out the expressions on what's left of the tiny faces. Other times I look for some subtle gesture of body language to reveal why they've come to visit me. I want to hear what their bodies have to say to me. I want to be able to offer them something, but what?

These babies, charred and voiceless, when they visit they break my heart.

Report from a Place of Burning

• • •

Carol was by yesterday. I could see her sorrow more than she usually lets me see it, and when I asked her what was up she ignored the question and acted frustrated at the messes I hadn't bothered to do anything about for days.

Look at these flies, she said, swatting at the air. How do you live with all these flies, Dad? she asked me, as if that was what had brought her all the way home. One or two flies.

Well, dear, I told her, I try not to judge them, lest I be judged. Carol rolled her eyes.

Really, dear, I've found that if I don't judge them and don't speak harshly to them or speak ill of them to others, they pretty much leave me alone. Oh, I told her, it's true occasionally one will alight on my arm or my nose and spend some time wringing whatever it has in lieu of hands, but that's rare and I just grin and bare it and as soon as I move or even just twitch it's gone.

Carol gave me that look I've seen from her as well as her sister, that look which says, Why do you have to be so strange, old man? They're filthy insects, Carol said, grimacing as she flicked a just-crushed one off her arm. They carry all sorts of diseases, and besides, she said, in that tone that let you know what was about to be said was the final word on the matter and not to be argued with, they're ugly.

In the eye of the beholder, I whispered, just loud enough for her to hear, carrying dirty plates out to the kitchen and the sink where others were already soaking. I winked and Dali, painting a mural on the walls of my living room, winked back. Carol couldn't see Dali or the mural. Too bad. She might like it. She's in it, after all.

Dali had been hanging out one day a few weeks ago when Carol had stopped by. When he saw her, the dead Dali literally fell to the ground, his Spanish knees collapsed under his body. Gala, he murmured from the carpet.

The Widower and Dali's Burning Giraffe

No, I'd told him. That's my oldest, Carol.

But he shook his head, his moustache continuing to move back and forth after his head had finished, so that the motion continued a little while along those long strands of hair. That, my friend, he said with his deep, Spanish accent, is the reincarnation of Gala, my wife, my inspiration, my demon.

Since then he's been furiously working on this mural in my living room.

Some nights he paints himself to exhaustion, which I imagine must be hard for a ghost to do. I wake up, having to go to the bathroom, and hear him snoring downstairs and sneak down to find him collapsed on the sofa with a brush still in his hand. In the mornings I hear him humming what must be Spanish ballads, feverishly at work on the mural.

Carol is the focus of his passion, that much is obvious from what he's painting. Her face appears in several different guises, on several different bodies. Only one of the bodies with Carol's face is actually her body, and that figure is the only undistorted, un-broken image in the entire landscape Dali has taken over my living room with. It's a beautiful likeness of Carol. It's her idealized, by Dali. Too bad she can't see it.

Out in the kitchen I heard water running. Carol was washing the dishes I hadn't gotten to in the last week.

So, Dad, she called to me from the kitchen, her hands, not the hands Dali was painting just then as if they were illuminated by some light from within but her real hands, picking up dishes and scrubbing at them with one of the green pads she found dried out on the counter. What do you think is the deal with all these babies being found burned in their cribs?

I didn't know what to say. Dali stopped painting, the hands unfinished, raw somehow. Dali turned from the mural to face me. There were tears moving down his face to drip from his moustache. His shoulders were shaking and he was sobbing, taking gulps of air in between sobs.

Report from a Place of Burning

I'm sorry, I said to him. I'm so sorry.

Dali turned back to the mural and walked into it and kept walking. Soon he was just a speck in the distance in that dream-like landscape, so tiny he could have been mistaken for an egg. Then I couldn't find his figure in the landscape at all, and then the mural was gone and the living room walls were just the living room walls again. And I still didn't know what to say to my daughter washing dishes out in my kitchen. I didn't know what to say to her at all.

• • •

In my bedroom I have a print of Dali's *The Burning Giraffe*. It's one of the things, Dali told me, that brought him by to visit in the first place. When I turn the lights out and get into bed, the light that comes through the blinds, from the street lamp across the street, lets me see the print, the aquamarine of the background a different hue than the bluish-gray tone of the dark room. I can just barely make out the figures of the women with their drawers opening, but the flames up the back of the giraffe in the distance reflect the street lamp's light in a way that almost makes those flames real flames. And the ghostly, pale figure I've often thought is walking toward the giraffe, toward the flames on the back of the giraffe, walking towards that fire as though it could offer him more than either of the women with their drawers and their red slab of meat in the foreground, at night, in the gentle touch of the street lamp's light, that ghost figure almost seems to be dancing. What, I sometimes wonder, falling asleep, just what is he dancing for? And who is he dancing with? And what is the music those flames are making on the back of that poor giraffe?

• • •

I don't know if Dali will come back or not. I want him to come back. I miss his sad and badly sung Spanish ballads in the morning. I miss the way that moustache of his continues his gestures after the gestures are done. I want him to come back. I want him to come back to finish the mural inspired by my oldest, the mural I'd come to think of as being titled *Apparition of Carol With Fruit Burning in Lorca's Mouth*. For some reason I believe that, were Dali to finish the mural, it would remain on the walls of my living room even after he leaves. It only disappeared when he walked off into it because it wasn't finished. Why do I believe that? Hell, I don't know. I mean, you have to be kind of foolish to believe anything at all, right? Besides, it makes sense. And, for the most part, the dead make sense. Certainly more sense than the living usually make.

I was talking about that just this morning with Sarah. This was this morning, not the past. The Sarah who comes to visit now and again, to sit with me and play cards late at night or walk beside me on my walks, the dead Sarah, is not the Sarah I sometimes find myself in the past with. The dead Sarah is older, and dead. The Sarah I find in the past is still living. Believe me, it's not possible to confuse them. Though they are the same woman, they couldn't be more different.

This morning I was talking with the dead Sarah about how it seems to me the dead have a better handle on things than the living do. She looked at me, when I said that, as if I had just pierced my tongue with a fork and had the fork hanging past my chin as I spoke.

Honey, you couldn't be more wrong, she said. She wanted to say more, I could tell, but instead she got up from the kitchen table and stood at the sink looking out the little window over the sink at some house sparrows that were flitting between the windowsill and the telephone lines sagging against what was a sky chock full of clouds.

This talking with the dead isn't as easy as you might think. There are times the dead clam up, and trying to drag more out of them just gets them angry. Though I wanted desperately to ask Sarah why she said that, about my being so wrong, this was one of those times, I knew, and I knew if I didn't change the subject Sarah would end up walking out the door and wouldn't come back for longer than I care to think about her not coming back.

So, did you see the mural Dali was working on in the living room? I asked her.

The one with Carol? she said, and nodded. Too bad he didn't finish it.

Maybe he'll come back and finish it. Maybe the next time Carol is over to clean up for me, I said.

Sarah, the dead Sarah remember, just shook her head, standing there looking out the window at the sparrows that still couldn't seem to settle on either the window sill or the telephone lines. Some things, she said, you don't get more than one chance with. Some things, she said, can't be finished.

Sarah never sounded sadder, dead or alive.

The Widow and the Magician's Ghost

HAUNTING IS NEVER CONSTANT. The dead, it seems, have the attention span of six-month-olds. They flit around us like befuddled insects. I wonder, do we do damage to the dead who are drawn to us? If the dead are fluttering insects, are we, the living, flames? Do we cause them pain they can feel but not understand?

Do we, the living, haunt the dead every bit as much as the dead haunt us? When we speak to them in our bedrooms late at night, do they have any choice or must they come to us and listen? Do the dead resent us interrupting whatever it is they do to come and sit or stand beside us and listen to us talk to them, those of us who can't seem to get past our needing to talk to them?

Maybe, and more and more I think this is the case, the dead can let the living go more easily than the living can let go of the dead. Maybe Ray, whose fingerprints might still haunt much of his handiwork around this house, maybe he's not so much with me as I am holding him back from being where he'd rather be. Is it possible, I wonder, for the living to be unfair to the dead?

How much does Ray, now that he's dead, know about me that I never let him know when he was alive and here with me and struggling to please me, to make me happy and keep me that way? Can the living keep secrets from the dead? Will the fear we can't keep secrets from the dead overcome my need to talk with Ray and let me sleep through the night finally? Should I ask Ray for some kind of forgiveness? What was it I put him through when he was alive and didn't know all there was to know about me? Is forgiveness something I need? Is it something Ray would grant me, if he could?

Maybe it's like the story of that magician, dead in his trunk under the stagnant water in the park in the center of town. No one thinks of the dead magician because the story is he got out of the trunk. Everyone who was there remembers to this day seeing him standing beside the tank, the trunk still submerged and bubbling in the water. Everyone remembers him taking the pale, delicate hand of his assistant and raising her arm with his and swinging it down in a final bow before walking off the makeshift stage. No one's sure what the magician did then, though some say they think they saw him get into a dark, late model Plymouth driven by a woman dressed in a dark fur, maybe sable. They say he kissed the woman before he snapped his fingers in front of her face and the car sped off, throwing gravel and dust behind it that floated in the air like the remnants of some magic act.

Others say the magician must have walked to the nearest liquor store, bought a bottle of twelve-year-old Tullamor Dew and found a motel room where he polished off the bottle and collapsed on the bed and was never seen again. The maid the next morning swears she felt like she was being watched as she changed the sheets on the bed and took the empty bottle out of the tiny waste can and put it in her trash bin. Once, she swears, as she bent down to work on one of the bottom corners of the top sheet, tucking it under, out of the corner of her eye, on the ceiling, she swears she saw the magician. The maid swears the magician winked at her and when she stood and looked up to see how he was clinging to the ceiling he was gone. Since that morning, the maid says, every time she goes in to clean that room, no matter who has stayed in it the night before, there is a single rose lying on the pillow of the unmade bed. It is the magician, she says. He leaves the flower for me.

The Widow and the Magician's Ghost

That's a story Ray would love. A dead magician leaving a rose on a pillow for a maid. With a story like that, no one's ever going to bother to look in the submerged trunk. Who would want to ruin such a story by finding the decayed remains of the magician in the trunk? Not Ray, that's for sure. And not me either, I guess. The dead magician, both confined and not confined within the rotting, submerged trunk, is a fair analogy for the forgiveness I don't want to have to ask Ray for if I don't have to. Secrets are messy things, it turns out. Especially ones that remain secrets till death do us part.

•   •   •

Has Ray been on the ceiling of Sam and Gloria's bedroom watching Gloria and I? And if he has, did it get him hard? Can ghosts get hard, and what would that mean for a ghost? Could a hard ghost be felt by someone alive?

What is it about men, that they get aroused by the idea of watching two women touch each other? Of course, alive, Ray never told me two women making love would excite him. Maybe Ray, if he has been on Gloria's bedroom ceiling one of the times we were together, maybe he wasn't turned on by watching us. Maybe he was just sad. Maybe he felt betrayed. Can the living hurt the dead?

Or is the thought of Ray on Gloria's ceiling nothing more than a representation of my guilt for never having been able to be honest with myself or with Ray while he was alive? Is it forgiveness I want from the dead, or simply acceptance? How much can the dead accept? I mean, they already have to accept being dead.

•   •   •

Ray is still so much with me sometimes. Once, holding Gloria as her breathing returned to normal and the red around her neck faded, I listened to her tell me about her childhood. She told me the story of her best friend in third grade. How, at the end of that year, on the last day of school, her best friend, Alice was her name, Alice told Gloria her parents had told her they would be moving in a couple of days. They had told Alice to say goodbye to her friends at school, because they were going far away and would not be back. Alice told Gloria she had not told anyone else, and had waited to tell Gloria because she knew that once she told her it would happen, and she didn't want it to happen. That day, as they waited for the bus with tears in their eyes and holding hands, Gloria said she felt like her heart was some sort of fish in her chest, kicking its tail furiously to try to swim off. Gloria said as the bus pulled up she took Alice's face in her hands and, before Alice knew what was going on, Gloria was kissing her. Gloria said at first Alice almost pulled away but then her lips pressed back and her mouth opened just a bit and Gloria said their tongues just touched and then Alice had turned away and was getting on the bus, waving to Gloria and smiling. Gloria said that kissing Alice that day had seemed the most natural and most wonderful thing to her. She had never forgotten that kiss. Gloria likes men, don't get me wrong. Still, the time she kissed Alice goodbye has haunted her all her life. Even now it haunts her. Am I, for her, a kind of Alice come back after all these years? It's not just the dead I'm afraid to ask things of.

Ray is still so much with me. After Gloria told me of kissing Alice, I told her a story. The story of how, when I was twelve, my heart stopped. I told her it was in summer, and I had just run out of the ocean and my mother was drying me with a beach towel. There were a couple of boys poking sticks at an unlucky jellyfish. Whether it was alive or dead they were too far off to tell. I told Gloria I remember hoping it was already dead so it didn't have to be suffering the boys' cruelty with the sticks. I told Gloria that was the last thing I remember thinking before my heart stopped.

My mother was still toweling me dry and I collapsed against her, into her arms, the towel enfolding me like wings. I told Gloria my mother started screaming my name and then she was yelling for my father who was still out in the water. I told her my mother told me later how she laid me down on the blanket and opened my little mouth and felt around in it with her fingers for anything that might be an obstruction. She was still yelling for my father as she pushed my head back so my chin was jutting out and up and pinched my nose with her fingers still wet from my mouth. She stopped yelling my father's name long enough to breathe into my open mouth. She said she was frantic.

My father, she told me, was beside her then, dripping on her back. He told her to move down and start pressing her hands down on my chest while he took over breathing into my mouth. My mother told me a crowd had formed around us there on the beach. I like to think even the boys had thrown off their sticks and were in that crowd, I told Gloria. I told her my mother said she and my father worked over me for what seemed like an hour but was probably only a matter of minutes, because, she said, when I finally took a breath on my own and then another and another, I was already fine. Even though my father picked me up in his arms and carried me off the beach to where our car was parked and put me in my mother's lap and got in the car and drove to the hospital, they knew I was fine. Though my asking them about the jellyfish, I told Gloria, did worry them a little.

I told Gloria that after that, I thought the dead were talking to me, that I heard them talking. I told her that, though my memories are a little fuzzy, I can still remember voices saying things to me, the oddest things, and often at times that were not good times to be listening to the dead. Like in school, when I was supposed to be taking notes on what the teacher was saying, suddenly I'd be hearing some dead person talking to me, and my notes became useless after that, a mish-mash of random thoughts and ideas and questions. I told Gloria I thought I could remember the dead talking to me right up until the time I met Ray. I told her that somehow just meeting Ray made the dead leave me alone. I told Gloria that was how I knew I loved Ray, that I loved him because he got the dead to shut up.

I don't know why I lied like this to Gloria. Like I said, Ray is still so much with me.

Report from a Place of Burning

Was I lying? Maybe that little girl whose heart stopped really was me. That's certainly as possible as me still now and then smelling vinegar in the air despite the fact the Heinz plant has been closed down for years. The stories we tell others even when we think we're lying might, it turns out, be true. Sometimes we just can't say for sure.

Maybe that's how my brother got lost. He was thirty-three when he was led out of the building where he had worked putting pieces of plastic together. Identical pieces of plastic. Over and over. Day after day. For nine years he had put those same plastic pieces together, the exact same way. Two men led him out after securing the straightjacket around him. By the time they got there, my brother had calmed down, but they still put him in that jacket. Procedure, he told me they said to him when he asked if they really needed to.

Sometimes, when Gloria and I are lying in her and Sam's bed and she has her arms around me from behind, holding my arms to my body and my body to hers, I pretend her arms around me are the sleeves of the straightjacket they carted my brother off in. I imagine Gloria is a straightjacket, but I don't struggle. Being confined that way, in my imagining of it, is a comfort.

Though I'm pretty sure it wasn't a comfort for my brother. Still, he had lost it, he told me, and at least three co-workers had to be hospitalized, one without two of his fingers. The straightjacket must have seemed a reasonable precaution, he told me later.

I visit him at least once a month. This is what can happen, Sis, he tells me, when the voices won't leave you alone. When the dead keep coming to you and talking your ear off and telling you to do things. Terrible things.

My brother has told me the dead are immune to all the drugs the doctors give him to get them to go away. When I visit him he's just my brother, and I tell him I can't understand why he has to stay in that place.

The Widow and the Magician's Ghost

I'm dangerous, Sis, he says. Or so they tell me.

You're not dangerous, I tell him. Just confused.

Once he told me Ray had been by to see him the night before. This was a couple of years after Ray died. It was his delusion at work. At least, I wanted to believe that. The thought of the ghost of my husband visiting what was left of my brother was too much for me to handle.

He asked me to give you a message, my brother told me. I watched while his forehead scrunched up like he was trying hard to remember the message exactly. The twilight zone, he said, my brother told me, isn't far off. My brother looked at me as if what he was about to say was a question he was asking me, and not something the ghost of my husband had told him to tell me.

I could have borne it, he said, my brother said.

•　　•　　•

Last night on the news another burned baby. Like the others, the police have no idea how it was done, or who did it. It's unreal, all these babies just going off in their cribs like Roman candles. And they say nothing else burns in the rooms. They say the inside edges of the cribs are charred, but nothing else. I've thought about going out and visiting my brother early this month. I've thought about asking him if he's heard anything about the babies, other than what he's heard when he's had television privileges. I've thought about asking my brother what the dead have to say about the babies burning up all over town.

Do they know who's responsible, I'd ask him. Is it one of them? I'd ask. Has Javed Iqbal come to town? I'd ask. Is the ghost of Javed Iqbal burning the babies, like he burned the pieces of the homeless children in acid after he had raped them? Tell me, brother, I've thought about saying, tell me what the dead know.

I've thought about it, but I'm not sure I want to know what the dead know. I'm not sure I want to hear what the dead have to say. I'm not sure why my brother is locked up and I'm still out here.

Report from a Place of Burning

At large, as they say. I'm not sure how much the dead have to say about us. The dead, too, are at large. Maybe the police don't stand a chance. No more than any of the rest of us do, left alive.

The Adulterer Curses the Static

WOMEN, IT TURNS OUT, are more adept at indifference than men have been led to believe. At least some women. Certainly Angela. And if Angela is typical, women are better liars than men, too. At least, they're better at faking emotion, which is supposed to be, after all, their domain. Angela certainly had me believing things it seems were never true.

I remember when Angela and her husband were going on a little vacation to points west. This was not long after the morality question became moot. Of course, the only reason anything happened between us was because I was already lost. I was so in love with Angela there was no way I could maintain my stance as a moral man when she asked me to kiss her one night in the ruins of the Heinz plant, which had become a kind of home for the two of us together.

Her home with her husband was a matter of maybe fifty yards or so to the east. In fact, from parts of the plant we could see the lit windows of the apartment where her husband was probably listening to police or fire reports over his broad band radio.

She told me he would sit in the little room he called a den, what was really supposed to be the second bedroom of their two bedroom place. He would sit in his den and drink beer and sometimes have some chips or something else to snack on, and listen to the faint and crackling reports for hours. The bastard would leave her alone for hours, until he needed more beer and didn't want to get up from his listening to go get it himself and would yell for her to bring him another beer, and she would. He'd stay in that den of his and leave her alone just so he could listen to pointless reports of small fires or break-ins or domestic disputes or, occasionally, a robbery or some violent assault.

She told me whenever she would look in on him he would be sitting in front of the radio, facing it and staring, waiting for the next static-broken report. She said she asked him once what it was he was doing, listening to those blurts of static and strained voices. She said he just looked at her like she had said something in some foreign language he'd never heard before. After a moment, he told her that by listening to those reports he was participating in the life of the community at large. He was staying up on what was going on. This, he told her, as if it were the last word that needed saying, is important.

Being with you, I told Angela when she told me this story, is what's important. How can he rather spend time listening to a damn police radio than to you? How can he not want to be touching you and holding you and making love with you? I just can't understand that.

That's what I told her, and I meant it. Angela is such an amazing woman. Her husband's apparent lack of interest in her is something I just will never understand. Of course, it would seem that she prefers his indifference to my passion. She's with him, after all. And pregnant with his child. And I'm alone, and stuck with training a new girl to take Angela's place, as her husband, after she started to show, decided, I guess, that it didn't look good, him letting her continue to work pregnant like that.

•   •   •

Not that he's interested in spending more time with her or anything. Even though Angela has decided we can't be lovers anymore, she still calls me at the store, and sometimes at home, to talk. It seems that even with her carrying his goddamn child he can't be bothered to pull himself away from his police radio or whatever else it is he does to stay away from her. At least, that's the way she presents things to me. At this point, I can't be sure how much of what she's telling me is the way things actually are. I can't be sure, in fact, of anything she ever told me.

Like that night before their vacation out west. We held each other, her in my lap, her legs wrapped around my legs, her head, when we weren't kissing, rested on my shoulder, and she talked about how she was going to miss me, and how I had to take care of myself, make sure nothing happened to me.

If anything happened to you, Angela told me, I'd be alone. I'd have no one to talk to.

You'd have your husband, I said.

She was quiet for a minute and rested her head on my shoulder. Then she kissed me and said, I'd be all alone.

Then she asked me to make sure to look at the moon every night while she was gone. She said every night she would look up at the moon and that the two of us both looking up at the same moon would make her feel closer to me. It'll be a kind of being together, she said, even though we're far apart. It'll bring us closer, she said.

Of course I promised her I would look up at the moon every night. I told her I'd take a walk every night, walking where we had walked together, and I would look at the moon.

It's odd, but there was one night she was gone that I looked up at the moon and it was nearly full and the face, you know the one you see in the moon when the light is right, well the face that night I swear looked just like Angela. The moon has never been so beautiful since. I convinced myself that the moon had Angela's face that night because we were both looking up at the moon at the same time. I told her that when she came back and she laughed and kissed me and we kept on making love, there in that place that had been ruined by fire.

Report from a Place of Burning

Was that it? Were the two of us ruined by fire too, or by the tearing down of the ruins of the Heinz plant by the ash-smudged men who come in for lunch most days? Is the indifference in Angela really ashes and smoke, or did the fire ever burn there at all? Maybe for Angela the fire never got near the town inside her. Maybe it was slowed and stopped by fire fighters long before it became more than a dim glow at night on the horizon. Maybe her husband listened to the chatter of the fire fighters through the static of his radio. Hell, maybe the people in the town inside Angela never even smelled smoke.

What's going on back there? I yell into the back, since there are no customers in the store. It smells like something's burning.

Under control, one of the cooks yells back. It's Tim, which lets me relax a bit. Tim knows what he's doing.

I used to be able to say I knew what I was doing. Angela fixed that. I used to be a moral person, a person who would never touch another man's wife.

Love has its own morality. Loving Angela made touching her not only a desire but moral. Not that that makes sense, not that it's reasonable. But then, love isn't reasonable. Or practical. Despite what Angela may have convinced herself of, in order to stay with her husband. In order to get pregnant with his child.

Angela would not, of course, agree with me, about the whole indifference thing. She doesn't see herself as being indifferent. She's just being practical.

He was there first, she's told me. As if linearity matters when it comes to the heart.

I want to make her see order has nothing to do with this. I want to tell her love isn't concerned with what others think. I want to close the store and walk over to the apartment where she's watching TV and he's in his den, calling for another beer, the static on that radio of his a history of indifference. I want to take her hand

The Adulterer Curses the Static

when she comes to the door to see who's knocking and, with a finger to my lips, I want to pull her out of that place of cold ash and distance and loss and take her home.

I would place her on my bed after taking off her clothes and spend the night massaging her legs and whispering a name to her rounded belly. In the morning the child kicking for the first time inside her would be our child, and she would kiss me and we would spend the whole day touching one another in bed and making plans for our daughter's future.

•   •   •

The books aren't balancing tonight. Something's wrong, and it looks like I'll have to stay late to straighten things out. Angela hasn't called. The kids up front are talking about another baby burned in its crib. I think it's up to eight now.

I'd tell whoever is going around setting babies on fire that cursing God doesn't work. I don't think he's listening.

Though maybe that's not it. Maybe it's just we can't curse loud enough to make it through the static.

The Mother Paints Cathedrals of Fire

NOTHING BUT THEORIES, that's all there is anymore. I try to believe it was different once, that there were at least a handful of certainties in the world, one or two things you could count on no matter what. Not this constant and absolute doubt; this is not how things have always been. I sense that, as if my intuition about tragedy is coming back to me. But I can't imagine what it must be like, having something you can trust won't turn on you.

Harlan, I know, worries about me. Sometimes, when I'm painting and he's at home, he sneaks outside so he can look in to the room where Samuel burned without so much as a whimper, the room now full of canvases in various stages, all of them pieces of one canvas too large to be contained by this small space, this space of fires in the midst of which his wife sits and works on one canvas or another. I can hear him as he steps carefully, trying to avoid making any sound, trying to go unnoticed.

He's not graceful, Harlan. He'd make an awful burglar. He's so awkward he'd end up in prison over and over and any neighborhood he was casing would be filled with people who would smile and wave to him, sure they and all their worldly possessions were safe so long as it's only him, Harlan the clumsy, Harlan the inept. Harlan the harmless.

The other night in bed I asked him why he sneaks outside to

look in to watch me paint. Why don't you just come in and sit down and watch? I asked him.

It doesn't seem right, he muttered, almost as if he were half-asleep. Then he turned over and grumbled something inarticulate and started to snore.

I wondered what it was that didn't seem right to Harlan. Him being in the room while I paint, or being in the room at all, him or me? Or did he mean that my painting what I'm painting in that room was what didn't seem right?

We used to communicate better, me and Harlan. Before Samuel left us, we talked all the time. About things that mattered. We talked about nonsense, too. And we laughed back then, too. Whatever Harlan meant, the statement stands and he's right. None of this seems right. None of it at all.

• • •

The canvas getting most of my attention lately is the center canvas of a triptych, the kind of series that, in the sixteenth or seventeenth century, would have been meant for an altar in some church where the prayers of people were connected to the fervent desire not to have to face the fires of hell. It would have been the center canvas for compositional reasons, not religious ones.

The fire in this one has just started to shatter glass. This is something I know about. A fire, left to burn within a structure, will fill that structure with gases, the oxygen and other gases burning, so an expanding bubble of heat builds around the flames themselves until the air around the fire is hotter even than the flames and at some point that heat produces a pressure that builds until glass, if it has not started to melt from the heat, shatters outward from the pressure. Shards of flaming glass burst out into the night.

In the painting I've been working on, the lower portion of a huge stained glass window is shattering from the fire. The upper portion of this composition of colored glass and lead bezels is starting to melt, the colors from the different portions of glass beginning to blur into one another, the lead bezels starting to warp out of shape from the heat. Whatever else the window once portrayed, only one clear subject remains.

In the one section of colored glass that isn't shattering or blurring into unrecognizable shapes, the baby Jesus raises his right hand in blessing. This Jesus has Samuel's face. His chubby hand is raised, the stubby fingers bent as if they had just let go of some rope that had tied everything in the world together and was now just ash at his feet or on the blue robe of the blurred Mary the Jesus baby with Samuel's face is seated on the detailed lap of.

The fingers form a complex figure that could almost be a letter in some ancient and extinct language. Or maybe not a letter but a symbol, the symbol for water perhaps. Maybe this baby Jesus with the face of my son who burned alone in his crib is trying to call to water to come and stop the burning.

I like to imagine some critic writing about the triptych, installed in some church in some other town, a town where babies don't go up in flames in their cribs. I like to imagine after he has gone on at some length about the beauty and the fury of the flames that consume much of the three canvases, the critic will focus on the role the baby Jesus plays in the mythology formed by the paintings. The critic will insist that everything, from the central placement of the child to the pattern of the shattered and burning glass below him, from the selection of colored glass, an illusion of the paint, an effect the critic will already have praised, to the blurring of color and the bending of shape going on around him, from the way the glass that comprises the body of the baby Jesus has a different feel than any of the glass surrounding him, *Almost as if, in the fiction of the image*, the critic will say, *the baby Jesus has a kind of fleshiness to it, as if that image is more real, more substantial, than any other figure formed of colored glass and lead*, from this kind of sacred earthiness of the child to the realistic texture of the flames, how all of this comes together in the critic's view to suggest fire is a kind of judgment, a morality even, in the world suggested by the three panels of the triptych, but a judging that the baby with the very real face on the Virgin's lap isn't prepared to make yet.

The child, the critic will go on to say, isn't Christ the condemner but Christ the healer, Christ the resurrector of the dead, Christ the resurrected. Despite all the ruin and the savage consumption that surrounds him, the critic will claim, this child offers those of us outside the painting, those of us not yet consumed by the flames but only singed, this Christ offers us the possibility of a life not governed by fire, not formed of pain and guilt and all the other punishments that often seem to be all there is for us in this world. Such hope, the critic will insist, is what the painter wants us to recognize and to cling to.

•   •   •

Harlan has begun hinting that maybe it's time I went back to work. We could use the money, he said the other night from the table while I was washing the dishes, my hands disappearing under pale suds reaching for the next plate.

I wanted to tell him of all the money the paintings will bring in when I finish them, but I just washed the next plate and reached back into the suds. He didn't push it. He never does.

But every now and then he slips, into some awkward conversation we're having, or, more often, into some long silence, some mention of money and our need for more of it. Or he'll mention the name of someone I used to work with, Carl say, or Gene, and wonder what they're doing these days. Harlan may be awkward walking around outside but he's got his own kind of grace when it comes to innuendo and suggestion.

It may not be fair, letting Harlan go off every day to his job out in the world while I stay in this house and spend my time painting these canvases of flame and madness. It may not be fair, but Harlan is not a mother. Harlan didn't carry our Samuel inside him for almost a full nine months. Harlan didn't feed Samuel with his own milk. I know Harlan loved our son, but love is only part of it for a mother, and I can't make him understand this. I don't have the words anymore.

It's all there in the paintings, whether or not Harlan or even my imaginary critic sees it. The paintings aren't just fires, after all. There are structures both containing the flames and being consumed by the flames. There are figures running through the flames, figures both on fire and not on fire. There are places the burning has not reached in some of the canvases, and there are other places that are all burning, nothing but burning. And all this burning isn't about ruin or devastation of one kind or another. There is both literal burning and a burning meant to be seen as symbolic, as suggestive of other ways we speak of burning. And not all burning consumes.

•   •   •

We haven't made love, Harlan and I, since the night I found Samuel charred and smoking in his crib. Oh, we touch, and we hold each other every night before Harlan drifts off to sleep and I turn over and lie there listening to his gentle snoring. He even kisses me when he comes home in the evenings from his time outside in the world. It's not that there isn't tenderness between us, or even desire. Though desire might not be the best word for what there still is between us.

It's not that it's the end of the world, I know that. All those murders in Uganda, for instance. That was nonsense, that kind of violence in the name of the coming of Christ for the second time. Those prophets and prostitutes offered their followers only loss. There's still more to the world than loss. Or at least I still want there to be more.

Harlan said something the other night I can't shake. Harlan was standing in the doorway of my studio, Samuel's old room. He was leaning against the door frame and looking around the room at all the various conflagrations. This is still a place of burning, he said and shook his head before turning away and heading off down the hall, where, in a few minutes, music started to play, something gentle and melodic on a saxophone.

• • •

Tonight the music is piano, and classical. Something by Mozart, I believe. My brush seems to want to move in rhythm to the concerto I can just make out. Though the piano is clear, the violins and other strings don't as easily make it this far. The music sounds incomplete. Though the piano is beautiful on its own, the music it makes longs for the accompaniment of the violins and violas and cellos. Still, it's enough, even alone like this, to give the lie to what I'm doing here, to make me think of turning my back to all this burning I've built up in this room where Samuel caught fire.

The music has been joined by the sound of a storm. It's a deluge, enough rain coming down with enough force to put out all the fires anywhere. No child tonight will catch fire in his crib, the sound of the rain coming down and the Mozart down the hall has me thinking.

I will put these brushes in thinner and clean the paint from my hands. I will take off these clothes spattered with paint and walk naked down the hall to where Harlan is listening to the piano insist that joy is possible even in this world. I will put my finger to his lips for silence as I undress him and slip him inside me as I settle over him, and the music will be inside us both and the rain will keep coming down in torrents.

Outside there will be worries of flooding. Inside me, Harlan will let go and, despite all the fires, life will start again.

The Detective Mute behind the Mirror

DeGreco insisted on going alone into the interrogation room the self-proclaimed prophet had been taken to. I want you behind the mirror, he told me, watching. One of us has to be out of the heat of that room, he said. DeGreco didn't call me kid. He was going into that room without me, but DeGreco trusted me to catch what needed to be caught. The heat, as they say, was on, and it was the two of us, together in this. I had to see what DeGreco would be too close to see.

DeGreco offered the prophet a drink. Coffee? a Coke? he said. The prophet smiled and shook his head. That smile of his could scrape paint, was my thought. It was the kind of smile you'd expect on the broad face of a used-car salesman on the one commercial he can afford. You've seen them, the local used-car lot ads that come on several times in a row around three in the morning. That kind of smile. Though what it was the prophet might have for sale I had no clue, and didn't think I wanted one.

DeGreco gave the mirror a quick side glance before sitting down across the table from the prophet, being sure to leave me easy access to the prophet's face.

Do you know why we asked you to come in today? DeGreco said.

Knowledge, the prophet said, smiling, is a rare and precious possession, best not taken for granted. What I might say I know is that an officer came to my current residence and made it clear I had no choice but to come with him, and it was this officer who brought me to this room and left me here alone until you came in. I also know that officer didn't know why he had been sent to bring me here. Beyond that, I could make some educated guesses about why someone wanted me brought here, but can I be said to know the reason for this particular coerced visit? To that, I would have to say, No.

The entire time the prophet was going on about knowledge and his lack of it in terms of DeGreco's question, what I noticed was the incantatory nature of his speech. There was a music just under the tone of his words that had a rhythm that was not the rhythm of what a man might say in response to being asked a simple, benign question like the one DeGreco had asked. It was more like the rhythm a primitive tribe of sun-worshippers might beat out, in an elaborate communal ceremony, on their tribal drums at sunset. This guy, this prophet, was no enigma; he wasn't even trying to hide that he was enjoying this.

Cute, DeGreco muttered. The mike picked up every sound in that room. I could even hear the sounds their clothes made when they moved. There have been times, with some suspects we were sweating, I could swear I've heard the beating of their hearts. Not with the prophet, though I was beginning to think I could hear DeGreco's heart and thought I should call the whole squad of detectives in and say, See, he does have one.

Okay, DeGreco said, let's get past the question of knowledge, then. Do you have any guess as to why you were asked to come down here today?

I hope, detective, I wasn't brought here to try to guess why you brought me here. That would seem to be an awful waste of time, especially when I gather you're under considerable pressure to, what is it they say, solve the case? DeGreco's arm pits and his back, I could see when he bent forward a little in his chair, were already dampening and the back of his shirt stuck a bit to his chair.

141

Report from a Place of Burning

Fair enough, DeGreco said. Are you aware that a number of babies have died recently, all in the same grisly fashion?

If you're talking about the babies found burned in their cribs, yes, I am aware of them, detective. What I don't know is why you brought me here to tell you I'm aware of something that's been on the local news almost every night. The prophet was most assuredly enjoying this, and was not going to hand us anything. DeGreco, at his best, would've had trouble cracking this guy, and DeGreco didn't seem to be anywhere near his best.

Do you know, sir, that some people are saying there's a connection between these babies and the legends of the red diver out in the gorge? DeGreco had lost me. I didn't understand why he was bringing this up. What I did notice was that DeGreco was sweating, and showed every indication of starting to let his anger take over. I had never seen DeGreco like this. DeGreco, it seemed to me, was losing it.

Really, detective? Are you telling me that the ignorant ruminations of the local rabble are being accepted as some sort of evidence by the police? If that is the case, the prophet said, then truly the world has gone mad.

Let's cut to it, shall we? DeGreco said. You and your followers claim we are living in what is called, I believe, the end time, correct?

First of all, detective, I don't have any followers, that I know of, nor do I make any claims. I am not the head of an organized church, or cult. I believe in what the Bible tells me, especially when things in the world reiterate what the Bible says. But unless things have drastically changed while I wasn't paying attention, belief in the teachings of the Bible is not a crime.

No, DeGreco said. Not unless that belief causes you to do something which is against the law. If that happens, then Bible or no Bible, you're still a criminal.

Ah, the prophet said, as if something had just occurred to him. You suspect me of having committed some crime. I assume, due to your previous comments, you suspect me of killing the babies in town who have burned in their cribs.

It doesn't seem completely out of the realm of possibility, prophet, DeGreco said. Religion has often been involved with the torture and slaughter of innocents. In the Old Testament, God tests Abraham by asking him to sacrifice his son to him, doesn't he?

Yes, detective, he does. But he also stops Abraham when it looks like he's actually going to do it. Remember, God sends down an angel to stop the knife coming down and the angel brings along a ram to be sacrificed to God. The slaughter of true innocents is a rarity when it comes to God's actions, the prophet said. No, detective, the random slaughter of innocents sounds more like the work of a man to me. Some very sick man, I'd say, detective. Wouldn't you agree?

Do you mean to ask whether I think God or man is sicker, prophet? DeGreco said. Wouldn't you agree that's a false dichotomy? I was trying to concentrate on the prophet's body language, what he might reveal, but where this interrogation had headed was making that difficult. What was this, a theological debate? Where the hell DeGreco was going with this, I couldn't say.

Wouldn't you agree, prophet, that since we are created in God's image, we share any sickness with our creator? That the sickness is within us because we are like God?

The prophet leaned forward, his smile the inescapable feel of dogma. What you call sickness, detective, seen from a different perspective, might be a kind of mercy, evidence of God's compassion, his love. Who is to say which view is correct?

When it comes to murder, prophet, I'll accept the responsibility for saying. A responsibility I'll gladly share with a judge and a jury. The rule of law, in other words, prophet. The rule of law.

Ah, but whose laws should govern us, detective, the laws of man or the laws of God?

The laws of man are derived from God, prophet. And I know of no conflict between them when it comes to murder, DeGreco said. Oddly, DeGreco seemed to have calmed down. Neither he nor the prophet were sweating under the hot lights in that room. And neither man was looking at the mirror. Tell me, prophet, why do you still swim in the gorge, despite the No Swimming signs posted?

Are you going to arrest me for swimming in the gorge, detective? How many years can I get for that?

Actually, it *is* against the law to swim there. But I'm not going to book you, prophet, for swimming in the gorge. But I am curious why you swim there. You must know it's bad for you. My ex told me not too long ago that our son got an awful rash from swimming there. What with all the chemicals that have been dumped into that water in the dead of night, it's impossible to say just how dangerous it is. So why take the chance, prophet? Why swim in it?

The gorge, if you must know, detective, is a sacred place for me. The prophet actually seemed a little nervous. It is a place of mystery and of signs.

And the red diver, prophet? Is the red diver a sign?

Do you not think it a little odd, detective, that a man would paint his entire body red and quote scripture before throwing himself into the gorge?

So, you were there when he dove into the gorge? I could tell DeGreco thought this meant something, that he was onto something.

Yes, detective. I was a boy, but I was there, and I remember him standing up on the edge of the highway and shouting scripture, and I remember him falling like some demented angel into the gorge and slipping under the water. You see something like that as a boy, detective, and it's kind of hard to forget. But what I believe the meaning of the red diver to be is personal, detective, something I don't share with others. I will say this, though. Read the Revelation of St. John. The red diver, as you call him, is there. I don't mean to claim that he's the only manifestation of that figure in the scripture. I believe the scripture reveals its truths to many of us, and the ways in which it manifests itself in the world is unique for each person.

And are the burning babies, prophet, some kind of sign? Are they in the scripture as well? DeGreco said.

The prophet's face, glowing under the hot lights, had a kind of faraway look. The prophet seemed as if he was no longer confined to that room with DeGreco.

Signs are signs, detective, whether any one is there to read them or not. Certainly you know that. Isn't your job all about the reading of signs? Only your signs, detective, are the clumsy signs of man. The signs I seek out are the enigmatic signs God sends us to let us know the time, as scripture says, is nigh. DeGreco was not going to get the prophet to admit to anything. All the prophet would speak of were issues of faith and God's laws, that much was clear to me. But DeGreco wasn't ready to give up.

So you're saying these burning babies are signs from God? De-Greco said.

If you're asking me as a believer in the word of God as put down in the holy scriptures, I'd have to acknowledge the possibility. Can I give you a direct correlation between these babies and the scriptures? No. But I will tell you this, detective. I do not believe the burning of these babies is a manifestation of anything within a man or a woman living on this earth. These little fires burning all over town are a mystery, detective, one you will not solve with your science and your powers of observation and deduction. DeGreco was lost. I could tell he thought the inconsistency he'd led the prophet into meant something, just as I knew he was wrong.

You're saying, prophet, you believe God is setting fire to these babies?

God, or his angels, the prophet said.

And you think God, or his angels, is killing these babies to provide a sign for someone to read? For you, prophet? Is God killing these babies to send you a message? What is the message, prophet?

Report from a Place of Burning

What is so damned important that these babies have to die horribly in fire to bring it to you?

The prophet shook his head. You operate from a false premise, detective. You speak of the babies as dying horribly, of them suffering for me. If it *is* God setting fire to these babies, the fire they burn in is a refining fire, detective, and the babies, they do not *suffer* God's fire. It is a kind of ecstasy, detective, a joy they are allowed to know briefly with their bodies but that they get to carry with them into heaven and to keep for all eternity. If God is burning these babies, detective, suffering, believe me, is not part of the deal.

DeGreco looked over to the mirror. Though he couldn't see me, I shook my head. Not enough, I was saying. We need him to say something about those arms crossed on the chests, something about the lack of physical evidence of any pain. All the prophet had said so far was he didn't believe God would make the babies suffer. DeGreco needed to find a way to push the prophet on this, to get him to slip up and say something about the condition of the charred corpses we hadn't released to the media, something only the person who had burned them could know.

Have you ever seen a victim of fire? DeGreco said. He knew he didn't have the prophet yet, I could tell.

I have seen many things, detective, both in this world and beyond it. There have been, you might recall, photographs published in the newspaper of the babies, though they weren't particularly clear or detailed photographs.

Damn, this prophet was good. Getting that on the record allowed him to say anything he might have seemed to know about the condition of the corpses came from seeing those photos in the paper. Though it's true we only approved a few, and they were photographs that didn't let you see much in the way of detail, that still gave him reasonable doubt and he knew it.

Fire, DeGreco said, is not a calm way to die. He wasn't giving up easy, I'll give DeGreco that.

The Detective Mute behind the Mirror

I wouldn't think so, either, detective, but I've seen movies taken during the Vietnam War of Buddhist monks setting themselves on fire as a form of ultimate protest, and I seem to remember them sitting there quite calmly as they burned to death. If a monk can stay calm as he burns, with just his faith, then surely, if it is God burning these babies, he can keep them from suffering in the burning, wouldn't you say?

So you do believe it's God setting fire to these babies? DeGreco said.

Actually, detective, I believe it is the work of angels, carrying out the will of God. And from what I've read in the newspaper, which I know can be suspect, everything seems to suggest that the burning of these babies is not a natural phenomenon. All the so-called facts of these cases, looked at objectively, leads to the conclusion that these fires consuming the babies are supernatural in origin. Yes, detective, I believe it is the handiwork of God, not of man.

DeGreco looked, through the slight tint the mirror gave the room, like a man who had been in one boxing match too many and whose brain had been battered around so much it couldn't tell him which way was up. He asked the prophet not to leave town without contacting the police first and told him he was free to go, but that he might have more questions for him in the future. The prophet smiled that oily smile of his, and DeGreco showed him out.

As he left with the prophet, DeGreco looked back at the mirror, and I knew that look was saying, I'm worn out, partner. You stay and keep at it and tomorrow, or maybe the next day, I'll be back and we'll start fresh. For now, the look said, I'm done here. The room was empty but for the bright lights the two men had burned under together. Those lights were too much. I had to turn them off.

Back in the office, the babies in the photographs seemed restless. I couldn't help but think of all their mothers around town, the empty holes burned in their futures. And I thought of the mother

of the fifth victim sitting in the nursery painting fires and humming a lullaby to her baby, who's beyond the touch of music on his
skin. The humming, I heard it so clearly I wondered at what the
imagination is capable of. Until I realized I wasn't imagining the
humming of that lullaby. It was me, humming again to the charred
babies pinned up around the room. The restless babies. Alone in
the office I hummed a lullaby to help them rest.

The Prophet and the Red Diver

THE RED DIVER OF THE GORGE came to me, finally, in a vision. At long last, he that had descended into the pit so long ago rose out of the murky depths of the subconscious, which is surely a manifestation, within each of us, of the pit. In each of us, the fires of hell burn, a carnival of sulphur and regret. We carry God's torture chamber with us every step of the way. Occasionally, visions manifest themselves as a side effect of this burden of our souls. The red diver dripped, in the vision, having just pulled himself out of the water. He stood on one of the large, flat stones around the gorge teenagers sun on. At first he didn't know I was there. At first, I didn't know I was there, though soon it became clear that my perspective in this vision was from my own body, that I was standing on one of the nearby stones.

The red diver rubbed the ragged wrist where his hand was missing, his body shaking. It may be it was only the cold air against his wet body, or it may be the red diver was crying. Visions are always ambiguous on some level. That which is the point of a vision, though, will be clear. Seeing his ragged, dangling wrist bone, I looked down at my own wrists, both leading to hands, and with this shift of focus became certain that I, my physical body, or rather the representation of it in this vision—was standing not far from where the red diver's body shook from sorrow or the cold. And once I knew I was there, so did the red diver.

Report from a Place of Burning

Someone, it might have been Jung, argued that we are every figure in any dream we dream. We posit ourselves, or different aspects of ourselves, as figures that take on representational value and become versions of who we are or who we wish we were. And dreams are first cousins to visions, one of the differences being that in a vision we are fully aware of our being in the vision and with this knowledge we gain a modicum of control. So, standing on what seemed to be a flat stone alongside the gorge, I knew I was there and that the red diver was also me, and so knew I was there because he knew what I knew. What aspect of me the red diver represented in this vision I still cannot say with certainty.

The red diver, aware I was standing so close to him, stopped rubbing his wrist covered with ripped flesh and reached inside the wound where his hand should have been as if there were something inside his arm he needed, something valuable he had been storing there. What he pulled out of his wrist was a small white stone. He held his one remaining hand out to me with the stone lying in its palm. It was clear the red diver intended for me to have the white stone. It was clear the stone was some sort of offering.

When I took the white stone from the red diver's open palm, my fingers felt the writing on the stone. The red diver's mouth was moving, but, as if this were a badly dubbed Godzilla movie, the timing of the words wasn't in synch with the movement of his lips.

And will give him a white stone, the mistimed voice intoned, and in the stone a new name written, which no man knoweth saving he that receiveth it.

I recognized the voice of St. John, his words. Thus the timing, or mistiming. The words of St. John had been placed in the mouth of the red diver, to be uttered to me in this vision in which I chanted the name on the stone, which, as I chanted, shivered its way into a different form, one that seemed, in the vision, oddly human. I chanted this secret name over and over and when I woke found myself saying the name over and over in the dark of my bedroom. This, I know, is my second name. The name I must take on after judgment. The name that is all there is to save me from the burning.

• • •

On the news tonight, on the Around the World in Sixty Seconds segment, they said that someone had stolen the skull of Pope Benedict XIII. The Moon Pope, he was called, in part because it is said he was quite mad. Why, you might ask, would someone steal the skull of a mad Pope. Who would do such a thing? you might ask.

Maybe the skull was taken by someone suffering one of our modern forms of madness and, in the midst of their particular delirium, they reasoned that, since it was the skull of a Pope, a Pope who was mad, if they could scrape the inside of the skull and ingest the scrapings while praying they might be cured of their madness by the residue of a Pope's madness.

Or maybe a woman stole the skull who wants only to break it open and breathe an air, a mad air, that has been trapped inside of that skull almost seven hundred years, believing, the woman, that by breathing this ancient breath of blessed madness she might be relieved of the guilt her body has accrued during a life lived in this fallen form of flesh. Desperation, that most common of all modern madnesses, rarely concerns itself with that process most of us would call reasoning. But when reason and madness come together, that, my brethren, is surely Biblical.

Maybe the man who took it believes the skull of the Moon Pope might, through the power of the madness it retains, be used to call the moon down out of the sky to purify this world of sin and despair. Maybe he will stand on the highest ground in Spain and, in a tortured Latin, chant to the moon, holding the stolen skull of the Pope up to the sky as if to offer it to the moon, to lure the moon down. And when the moon comes down to lick the sunken eye sockets of that bitter skull of a mad Pope, the oceans will rise to cover all the earth, the moon, and the mad man holding a Pope's skull.

Report from a Place of Burning

Or maybe this mad skull of a Pope is in a crate, having been stolen by a woman who is bringing it home with the hope that it may be used to cure this town where babies are going up in flames in their cribs. Maybe she believes the madness still housed in the ancient cavern of the skull will be able to counter what she takes for the madness she believes to be responsible for the deaths of the babies and, joined with the right ceremony, with the proper prayers, the skull can cleanse the town of the stench of these tiny, charred figures of death.

Of course, it's possible whoever stole the mad Pope's skull is not interested in madness at all, but in death.

In those days, St. John wrote, shall men seek death, and shall not find it, and shall desire to die, and death shall flee from them.

Maybe the thief believes the skull can offer some power over death, can chase death off, make it whimper and curl up in a fetal position and forget what it is.

What might not be contained, after all, in the skull of a long-dead Pope, especially one like Pedro Martini de Luna, who believed he was a second Noah? Alive, and Pope, Pedro had been known to stand naked on the parapets of his family's castle on an island just off the coast of Spain and, having shed the miter and the robes that defined him not as a man but as Pope, raise his fists to the night sky yelling at the moon in a voice some who heard it claim was not his voice at all. They say it was deeper and full of a foreign sound. And some say the moon, it yelled back at Pedro. That Pedro and the moon would go on like that for hours, yelling in what seemed to be a kind of guttural Latin back and forth.

It is said, too, that Pedro's naked flesh was scarred in ways that echoed the scars men of science, looking through contraptions of steel and ground glass, were saying they saw on the moon. One woman, a maid-servant who had been with the mad Pope more years than anyone else, believed the arguments Pedro had with the moon were the typical troubles between a father and son.

Some say that, on nights the moon is full and rises large and orange over the walls of the castle Pedro was finally banished to, stripped of his name and title, if you listen you might still hear the faint echoes of Pedro and the moon screaming a demented Latin at one another.

•   •   •

What might the skull of a Pope who argued with the moon in Latin have to say to death? Could such a skull, with the echoes of the body and all its sins and the memory of the miter's weight upon it, understand the nature of death in ways other skulls cannot? Could a Pope's skull recognize signs of the coming of the end of things more readily than a living Pope? How much memory of the flesh can bone carry forward? And, after centuries, is there even one Latin word left the skull hums as wind passes through it? Is it a blessing or a curse, that one remaining word, if it's there at all? Was the skull stolen by a woman or a man, or is the disappearance of this skull that might act as a sort of Geiger counter for the end of things a sign?

If I had the skull of the Moon Pope in my hands, what would it have to say about the embrace of Bracha Genossar and her daughter, Ariela McCary, found swaying in a kind of dance with death under a ceiling beam in the family room? With the right music, their bodies, held together by arms stiff with rigor mortis, could have been said to move with a kind of grace both undeniable and mysterious. Let down from their posed last dance, the paramedics had to break their arms to pry the two women apart.

Would the skull say it was not one another they had embraced, but that figure that danced all their lives with both women, held between them by all four of the women's arms, that figure whose name is the loneliest and longest single syllable of all?

Would the skull of the mad Pope just grin at the boy in Helena, Montana whose heart was pierced by a pencil, who felt the pencil go in but said it didn't hurt and yelled for his mother, telling her he was going to die. The pencil stuck in his chest throbbed with

153

his pulse as if directing some ghostly orchestra playing some long funeral dirge.

Though the orchestra of the dead played perfectly for him, the boy didn't die. Maybe the skull of the Moon Pope who went by Pedro would sing a hymn with that ghost orchestra to the rhythm of that throbbing pencil in the chest of a boy on his birthday in Montana.

The skull, wherever it is, isn't asking for anything.

•   •   •

Skulls, whether the skulls of Popes or of men who have made their flesh into signs the church all but ignores, are empty cages of bone. To hold such a thing in one's hands and place a kiss upon the ridge of bone over the teeth is a ceremony of loss. The taste of loss is the taste of dust on bone, or the taste of the damp and rotted remnants of skin floating loose in dark water around the gash of a mouth.

Yes, I kissed the corpse of the red diver in the gorge. And this was no dream, no vision. The vision just let me know it was time for me to go to the gorge and dive in and dance with the lost body of the red diver.

It was I, the only one who witnessed the fall in its entirety so many years ago, tied to that fence, I who, swimming, the vision running in my memory, the murky and foul water that fills each year the gorge, bumped into something swollen and stiff and floating, one hand ripped off so long ago. After I had brought the body back up and laid him out on a rock to dry, I swear a thin, bluish smoke began to gather and drift up out of the wound that should have been a hand.

And the smoke of the incense, St. John wrote, which came with the prayers of the saints, ascended up before God out of the angel's hand.

And that thin scrawl of blue smoke caught in a wind and pointed to where the sun was half-obscured by some cloud whose shadow draped itself over the landscape in the direction of town. The coming storm, I thought. Whatever gases had waited inside the body of the red diver all those years in the foul water of the gorge had no more wait left in them. The scrawl of blue smoke rose up, leaving the red and rotted flesh behind, and curled and twisted itself into a name. The name my finger first felt on the white stone in the hand of the dream-corpse of the red diver. The name I believed was the name that, uttered, would save me from the time of despair after the judgment.

And then the smoke took on the figure of a lamb, whose bleating sounded like the sound, in my nightmares, of the flesh of a five-month-old baby burning, layer after layer of skin letting go the gases that wait just below them.

And then the smoke was no more than the faint residue of the ash of the lamb burned in sacrifice and sifted over the earth.

Sitting beside that bloated, crimson body, the tattoos burning my thighs almost to madness, I alone heard the voice of He that sat upon the throne saying, *I make all things new.*

Signs are signs, with or without faith.

Signs are signs with or without a text to contain them.

Soon it will all be moot. Soon the thousand years will begin, and the deaths of less than a couple of handfuls of babies will pale before the deluge to come, though they died by the fire and by the smoke and by the brimstone which issued out of the mouths of angels.

Behold, I come quickly, St. John says out of my mouth. Blessed is he that keepeth the sayings of the prophecy of this book.

The Widower Dances

On the news tonight, near the end, in the local report, there was talk of a rumor someone pulled a body out of the gorge. The cute reporter, who reminds me a little of Sarah, before the cancer, who was obviously standing on a stone near the scum-covered water in the gorge, reporting from the scene as it were, said someone called in a report, on their cell phone, claiming to have seen a guy in a swimsuit carrying what looked to be a red body, in his arms, out of the gorge.

The red body, the caller said, according to Sarah's look-alike, looked bloated and was dripping water as the man in the swimsuit carried it towards a gray, beat-up Pontiac parked on the side of the road near the gorge. If it hadn't been for the condition of the body, the caller said, looking a little embarrassed when interviewed later by the cute reporter, he might have just taken it for two lovers sneaking back out of the gorge after going for a swim. The man in the swimsuit was carrying the red body with a tenderness that suggested a kind of intimacy, the caller said. In fact, just before he put the red body in the trunk of that waiting Pontiac, the caller said, the man kissed what must have been its putrid and bloated lips.

The cute reporter, the camera focused again on her, vestiges of the gorge just visible surrounding her centered face and a bit of her shoulders, said the caller couldn't be sure about what he reported, since he'd witnessed this while driving by some seventy yards or so from the county road by the gorge where the Pontiac was parked.

Oddly enough, she went on, eighteen years ago, there had been a report, substantiated at the time by a number of witnesses, that a screaming naked man, who had painted his entire body red, had leapt off the old interstate bypass into the gorge. They dragged the gorge for his body, she said, but never found it. There is a story, though it may just be a kind of urban myth, local legend as it were, she said, that they did come up with his hand, ripped off at the wrist, and that yes, it was red. Someone at the local college is said to have put the red hand in preservative and stored the jar away. But when I asked the chair of the Biology Department today, she said, she told me no one has seen the jar with the red hand floating in it for years.

Could it be, she said into the camera, as if she were talking directly to me and not every other person watching the 5:30 local news, that someone today pulled the body of that red diver out of the foul water of the gorge?

The camera cut back to the interview with the caller, which had apparently been done in the caller's home. The caller seemed to be sitting on a couch and behind him, off to the left, there was a painting. It was a little out of focus, but it looked like it was some four-legged animal on fire and running towards the foreground of the canvas.

What do you think it was you saw? the voice of the cute reporter said, off camera.

I can't say for sure, the caller said. But there was nothing natural about it, that's for damn sure.

• • •

After the news, I had to go for a walk. After all, Dali still had not come back and so the walls in my living room were just bare, white walls.

Report from a Place of Burning

A Pontiac, gray but not beat-up, drove by and in the backseat, looking at herself in a little hand-held mirror, the kind Sarah used to carry in her purse for what she liked to refer to as emergencies, though I never understood what kind of emergency she meant, was Marilyn Monroe.

Once I asked Sarah if by emergency she meant some kind of medical emergency where she'd have to use the little mirror she'd pull out of her purse to check if some victim of some sort of attack or another was still breathing. She looked at me as if she thought I was just trying to be funny and failing, and didn't answer.

Marilyn was apparently just putting the finishing touches on her pouting lips. All she was wearing, this dead Marilyn Monroe, at least as far as I could tell, was a see-through black negligee of some sort, with what was either black fur or black feathers along the neckline which draped low over her breasts.

Quite fetching, I whispered.

Marilyn looked over to me as the Pontiac went past and pursed her lips as if to blow me a kiss.

· · ·

Without planning it or even being aware of it, I made my way to the street with the house in which I knew a baby had burned in its crib, the one Darrel had questioned me on my motives for walking by the night after the baby had burned there. The yellow police tape had long since disappeared. There was nothing to distinguish that tragic house from any other, nothing to mark it as different from the house where Sarah and I had listened to a couple make love.

I needed to talk with Sarah, but I was alone.

As I got close to the house, I looked toward the second floor window, the one I had always assumed to be the window of the baby's room. I'm still not sure I saw what I think I saw. If I did, what I saw was a naked man, painted red, holding the naked body of a baby in his red hands and dancing with the baby around the room. Though I only saw the apparition a few seconds, it seemed real, and it seemed as though the baby was laughing out loud while the red man grinned and swirled around the room that was filling with smoke and that must have already been filled with music. Out where I was there was no music to dance to, and no reason to dance, as far as I knew.

Standing in front of the house, that second-floor window was as dark and empty as all the other windows, and I remembered some of the local myths that had sprung up concerning the figure of the red diver. Like the one that said all the burned babies, every one of them, had been fathered by the red diver come out of the dank water of the gorge to lie with local women and give them his seed. That it was his parentage of them that caused them to flame up in their cribs in their sleep, tiny little bursts of a sort of prophecy. Signs of what is to come, perhaps.

If, I said to the house in a whisper, the red diver's lost body has been found, may that mean an end to this season of burning babies.

Yes, it was a prayer I whispered standing in front of that house. A prayer for the babies, and their parents, that might still go up in flames alone, or not alone, in the middle of the night.

●　　●　　●

The dead, it seems, may not be up for visiting tonight. Other than Marilyn, who was on her way elsewhere and only paused to blow me a freshly lipsticked kiss, I've been on my own all night. And I haven't found myself in the past for what seems like months, though it may only be weeks.

Though it's Sarah I really want to talk to, I'd settle for just hearing Dali's awful voice singing some Spanish ballad in the living room while he painted Carol's hands as if they were a religious icon. This house, like my daughters have both said at different times, does seem empty tonight. It's awful empty, this house, without the dead.

Report from a Place of Burning

•   •   •

I was slicing up an apple for a late night snack when I heard Dali singing in the living room. My Spanish isn't good, but I've picked up a little. The ballad he was singing had to do with a deer that housed the spirit of a beautiful woman who had died giving birth. The gods, what gods they were I couldn't tell but whatever gods they were, had taken pity on this woman. Because of her beauty, of course.

Because of her beauty the gods had let themselves feel her sorrow at having to leave her child alone in the world. The gods found themselves, so the song went, weeping for the woman's pain and loss. Their remedy was a remedy that only a Spanish ballad sung by a dead surrealist would have come up with, gods or no.

The gods put the soul of the woman in a deer, and in that deer the gods let the memories of the woman run on all four thin and graceful legs through the forest near where the wife's mourning husband raised their daughter alone as best he could.

Translation is a tricky thing, but I think the gist of the song is that the mother, in the form of the deer, befriends the child and in that way is able to watch over her as she grows up. And this mother in the deer is just outside the bedroom, with its windows open for the deer's sake, when her child, now a woman, gives birth to her grandchild. As the girl child is born, the ballad says, the deer outside folds its legs under its body and places its long neck and chin on the ground and breathes its last breath. The Spanish are still so romantic.

With Dali singing and painting in my living room, I felt a little better. And my mother was with Dali. When she saw me, the last slice of apple in my fingers poised in front of my lips, my mother waved and smiled as she pinched Dali's left butt cheek. Dali jerked and laughed, throwing his arms, the brush still in his pale right hand, around my mother and kissing her with that Spanish passion of his.

The Widower Dances

. . .

Sarah, it turned out, the dead Sarah not the Sarah of the past, was waiting for me in bed, wearing the same black negligee Marilyn had had on in the back of that Pontiac. How long she'd been lying there in that see-through number I couldn't say, but I was glad she was there.

How was your walk? my lovely dead wife asked me, smiling like she knew something she couldn't wait to tell me.

I reached for her and she put her hands into mine and let me pull her out of the bed and put my arms around her. It was a wonderful night, I told her, for a Moondance, and then we were dancing in the dim light of the full moon coming in through the window.

For a moment I wondered what someone walking by on the street and looking up to the bedroom window would see. Would they see a man with his arms holding nothing at all dancing by himself around this room, or would they see a man holding a woman in a beautiful negligee dancing in a way that made it clear they had done this many times before, that each knew how the other moved as well as they knew their own flesh?

Would what they saw, whichever it was, be enough to shatter their lonely heart, if their heart were lonely?

As we danced, Sarah and I, and she hummed "Moondance" into my ear, I believed the season of burning babies was over, that no more babies would be found charred and smoking in their cribs. The red diver's children were with their father, I thought, and whoever had torched those innocents was finished with fire.

I danced with my dead wife, and it was perfectly natural.

The Author

George Looney's books include *Hermits in Our Own Flesh: The Epistles of an Anonymous Monk* (Oloris Publishing, 2016), *Meditations Before the Windows Fail* (Lost Horse Press, 2015), the book-length poem *Structures the Wind Sings Through* (Full/Crescent Press, 2014), *Monks Beginning to Waltz* (Truman State University Press, 2012), *A Short Bestiary of Love and Madness* (Stephen F. Austin State University Press, 2011), *Open Between Us* (Turning Point, 2010), *The Precarious Rhetoric of Angels* (2005 White Pine Press Poetry Prize), *Attendant Ghosts* (Cleveland State University Press, 2000), *Animals Housed in the Pleasure of Flesh* (1995 Bluestem Award), and the 2008 novella *Hymn of Ash* (the 2007 Elixir Press Fiction Chapbook Award). He is the founder of the BFA in Creative Writing Program at Penn State Erie, where he is Distinguished Professor of English and Creative Writing, Editor of the international literary journal *Lake Effect*, Translation Editor of *Mid-American Review*, and Co-Founder of the Chautauqua Writers' Festival.

CPSIA information can be obtained
at www.ICGtesting.com
Printed in the USA
BVHW03s0753110818
523774BV00009B/10/P

9 781948 585002